The Unforgettable Sheikh
Ultimate Billionaires Book 4

Barbara McMahon

The Unforgettable Sheikh
Copyright © 2017 Barbara McMahon
All Rights Reserved

One

Sheikh Karif bin Shakirah!

Chloe stared in stunned fascination at the familiar face staring up at her from the glossy photograph she'd just been handed. After all these years--

Her heart jumped. She caught her breath. *It was Ben!*

A flood of emotions swept through her—heartache, nostalgia for what might have been, a strong feeling of abandonment she'd lived with for so long.

But foremost was the anger that flowed surprisingly intense and hot and fresh. It'd all happened ten years ago, yet she felt it as if it had been yesterday. Blast him!

Today she'd see him again. Her heart pounded in her chest. Would he speak to her? What could he say that would make any difference?

She traced her finger along the edge of his jaw, almost feeling his heat, as if he were real instead of an image in a glossy black-and-white photo.

Wishing she could rake her nails on that flawless skin, aching to hurt him as much as he'd hurt her, anger roiled within as she clenched her jaw. After all this time, shouldn't the intensity have faded?

"You okay?" Mike asked, perched on the edge of her

desk.

Chloe blinked and looked up, consciously relaxing her muscles. It was only a picture.

"Sure. Tell me again about this assignment." Resolutely she kept her eyes on the face of the news journalist in front of her, though she longed to study the picture. Longed to see how the years had treated him.

"I knew you weren't listening. Paul was going to cover the event. He's been working on the prelims all week. But his wife went into labor and you know Paul's determined to be there with her, so we get the job. This sheikh's meeting with the president will be reported at ten on the lawn since no rain is forecast. It'll just be the usual goodwill-between-nations garbage. But the boss wants to get some pictures. Any country willing to give the U.S. first crack at its oil reserves without going through the cartel gets a lot of positive press."

Mike shrugged. "You take good pics, I'll try for a one-on-one interview or some new angle to appease the boss."

Chloe nodded, her eyes drawn irresistibly back to the photograph.

"What do you know about him?" she asked. She searched the image for signs of the man she'd once known, curiosity rampant.

He'd disappeared from her life without a word. She hadn't even known if he was dead or alive. Somehow, she'd come to think him as dead.

But the picture portrayed him in the best of health.

A feeling of betrayal blossomed. For years she'd wondered, worried, mourned. What had happened to him? They'd been so in love--or so she'd thought. They'd even discussed marriage.

Then he'd vanished without a single word.

What changed? Why hadn't he at least told her goodbye?

Mike reached for the file he'd handed to her. "I don't know much about him beyond what's in here. I'll read on our way over. Knowing White House security, we won't be allowed too near until the official end of the dog and pony show. Who knows even then his own bodyguards might not want the press too close."

"I do know my part," she murmured absently.

She ought to, she'd been doing it long enough. The questions now were did she want to do this shoot? Dare she do this shoot? Could she calmly focus her camera on Sheikh Karif bin Shakirah when she would rather fling it in his face?

Could she do her job and walk away without giving in to the urge to vent some of her seething anger?

"Yeah, yeah, I know. You're Mason's fair-haired child. Can't do anything wrong," Mike said easily, referring to their boss.

Chloe grinned at that remark and tossed the picture aside. Meeting Mike's teasing glint, she wrinkled her nose at him. "You're a great one to talk. Who's up for a Pulitzer Prize?"

"So we're both his fair-haired children. Come on, traffic will be a nightmare. We'll be lucky to get there before the event's over, much less before it starts."

"You drive," Chloe said as she began to gather up her equipment.

She could do this, she told herself. She was a

professional. She'd take several lenses, a dozen filters. Not that she planned to use all of them, but she liked to be prepared.

She'd tried hard over the last decade to anticipate every turn of events in her career as well as her personal life so she'd never be caught as surprised and unprepared as she'd been ten years ago.

"I wanted you to drive. I have to read the background," Mike protested.

"I'll read it to you," she said, throwing her bag over her shoulder.

She was used to the weight of the camera. She felt comfortable and confident in her ability. She'd been in Washington long enough to acquire the coveted White House coverage for the paper. She knew some of the security guards personally, some of the current administration's staff.

What she didn't know was how she'd react when she saw Karif in person after all these years. She suspected she'd want to rant and rave and throw something.

Instead, she'd take a bunch of pictures and leave. She tilted her chin in determination. She'd live through this. She'd lived through far worse.

Karif bin Shakirah accompanied the president out into the sunshine. The deep green lawn had been recently mowed and the smell of fresh-cut grass lingered in the warm air. There was a slight tang of exhaust fumes from the traffic not seen but heard far beyond the grounds. The humid air carried the sultry fragrance of the flowers blooming so profusely. He savored the various aromas so different from those in his homeland.

The distance to the barrage of microphones was short. Dignitaries and staff members from both nations followed. Several dozen were already waiting in front of the microphones in the chairs provided or standing to the sides. Security was tight. Karif noticed both uniformed and non-uniformed personnel, but the openness of the setting was typically American.

He liked America and was glad to be visiting again.

Karif was also satisfied with the just concluded breakfast meeting. While primarily a rehash of the negotiations that had been conducted over the past months, neither side had anticipated any major changes. And there had been none. His visit was one of goodwill and friendship--and financial gain for his own country.

For Karif the visit to the United States was special. For the first time in ten years he was back in America. He planned to take a vacation after the treaty was signed--linger in the States while his ministers returned home.

He was going to start in Berkeley. His plans beyond that depended on what he learned there.

For ten years he'd thought about Chloe McDonald. He'd tried to locate her in the months following his departure--only to find she'd left Berkeley and virtually disappeared.

Depending on others to locate her had proved unsatisfactory. Now he knew why earlier investigations had proved worthless. This time he was going to see what he could discover for himself. No one would stop him.

A slight breeze blew his burnoose behind him. He

adjusted the formal caftan and came to a halt beside the president in front of the mikes. He and the ministers that had accompanied him wore their desert garb proudly. It represented their country and gave the cameramen a good show, he thought cynically. Western attire would have suited him; it was more and more the norm in his country these days. But he bowed to custom and protocol. And the expectation of the American public.

The Washington Monument towered in the distance, gleaming white in the morning sun. From the White House lawn, Karif saw the crowds already queued up around the base of the obelisk. He'd like to go up in it but doubted it would be possible this trip. Maybe he could slip back into town after his West Coast venture--return incognito, as he had lived in Berkeley.

He cherished his memories of his time at the California university. Not all of them centered around Chloe, though most of them did. The old, almost-forgotten frustration rose. What had happened to her? Where had she disappeared to? What had she done with her life? Had she forgotten him?

His eyes drifted around the crowd as the president made his opening speech and introduction. Idly, Karif studied faces, wondering who he'd meet at the various functions being held over the next week in his honor and who were in attendance today because he wouldn't meet them later? Who was important to the future welfare of his country? Who was milking the event for personal gain?

The press was to the left of the seated dignitaries, behind a taut rope. Photographers snapped pictures. Men and women spoke softly into handheld recorders, or scribbled on.

Karif's gaze focused on a young woman hidden behind a camera. For a moment, he thought he recognized her. Was it only because he was in Chloe's country? Only because he'd been thinking about her that he saw Chloe in the tall, brown-haired woman?

The camera focused on his face. He could see the photographer's finger snapping exposure after exposure. The woman dropped the camera and for one startling moment Karif's gaze locked with hers. Then she dropped her gaze to her camera as she coolly changed a lens.

It was Chloe!

Stunned, Karif stared at her. While he believed in fate and in the karma that guided everyone's lives, he'd never expected to find her so easily. His first trip to the United States in a decade and he was at the same place as Chloe.

His lips tightened and his eyes narrowed. Was it possible? Was that truly her?

As soon as the ceremony was completed he'd send Salid to escort her through the barrier. He'd wanted to talk to her so many times. Discover why she'd disappeared from Berkeley. Find out what she was doing .

Had she married?

For a moment, anger threatened to flare out of control.   He was not the man he'd been ten years ago. Circumstances had changed and the past couldn't be changed.   But he still felt the blazing anger at what had transpired..

"—present Sheikh Karif bin Shakirah," the president concluded with a smile as he turned to face Karif.

The smattering of applause recalled Karif to his reason for being there. For a split second he almost forgot his speech, almost forgot his country, the reason for his visit.

He wanted to call across the open space and demand Chloe leave the press section and join him to make sure she didn't disappear from his life a second time.

But thirty-four years of training held sway. Calmly, Karif stepped up to the microphone and began his speech, thanking the president for his invitation to visit then extolling the virtue of the proposed treaty. He gave his speech without referring to notes, without hesitation for a single word. His command of English was perfect, if a bit influenced by his British schooling.

From the nods of his fellow countrymen and the pleased looks in the audience, he knew he was saying what everyone wanted to hear. But his mind was churning with thoughts of the photographer only a dozen yards from him.

Chloe.

He turned to offer his hand in friendship to the president conscious of the constant click click as dozens of cameras recorded the event. Smiling formally, nodding, speaking clearly for all to hear, Karif wanted nothing but leave all this behind and pull Chloe into some secluded corner to find out what she'd been doing since he last saw her.

How long would this display continue? How long before he could get away and talk to Chloe?

When he turned to look for her again, she was gone. He searched the press section—in vain. She wasn't there.

He returned his attention to the president. There'd be time enough later to find Chloe. He now knew where to start looking. He needn't wait until his official visit ended. If it took his entire stay in Washington, he'd find her.

Stupid, stupid, *stupid!* Chloe berated herself as she banged her fist impatiently on the steering wheel. The last thing she needed was Mike asking a thousand questions when he joined her. He'd wonder why she'd dashed off so quickly, ask what she thought about the honored visitor, how her pictures had come out. The last thing she wanted was an inquisition.

Her nerves were stretched too taut for that. She should have stayed in the press section until the other journalists were ready to leave. She should have mingled and exchanged small talk as she normally did.

Of course that is what she should have done.

But she hadn't. She couldn't.

Not after Karif recognized her.

She shivered as she relived the moment his gaze locked with hers. His dark eyes had been unfathomable. She gleaned nothing from his expression. But the jolt of anger that had shaken her was stronger than ever. She couldn't chance a meeting.

Not daring to trust herself, she fled for the safety of the company car.

She longed to drive back to the office and upload the pictures to see which ones they'd use in the next edition. The images she'd taken seemed to burn through the camera--she wanted to get rid of them.

Though she wouldn't be able to get rid of the images in her head as easily.

Sheikh Karif bin Shakirah. She believed she'd known him ten years ago, had thought they'd shared something special. She'd never loved anyone as much as she'd loved him.

Yet he had never once hinted at his true identity.

A sheikh! How ironic. She thought him wildly romantic and endearing when they'd known each other at Berkeley. He'd been so special, that tall, dark man who spoke with such a charming accent. Who seemed delighted in the simplest of pleasures. Who had relished the rowdy sport of football with the same enjoyment he'd shown at the ballet and the symphony.

She had thought him just another college kid.

Taking a deep breath, Chloe tried to calm her rioting senses, quell the intensity of her emotions. That was in the past. A decade ago. She was never going to fall for some heart-stoppingly handsome man again—ever! She'd learned her lesson, hard as it'd been.

Just because his eyes looked like liquid ebony with starlight shot through was no reason to feel soft and mushy when he looked at her.

Just because he still had that adorable dimple in his left cheek when he smiled was no reason for her knees to turn to jelly. He meant nothing to her. Less than nothing after his betrayal.

Just because her pulse still pounded from being so near him was no reason to think she wasn't totally in charge of her emotions.

She was a competent career woman, no longer some silly impressionable naive teenager. She'd built a good life for herself and her daughter, Mackenzie. She refused to fall prey to mere sexual attraction again. She refused to be drawn into any man's orbit deluding herself that it was love.

Who was she trying to kid?

She'd been crazy in love with Karif. Loved everything about him, from his odd sense of humor to his enchantment with everything American. She loved him long before she'd shared her body in love.

They'd talked of marriage. He'd said it might not be easy, but they'd work it out together. She thought he loved her in return, that the difficulties had to do with their different cultures.

In truth they were a world apart.

She hadn't really known him at all. She hadn't known he was a sheikh. She hadn't even known his full name. He deliberately let her think he was an average foreign-exchange student attending the university.

"Where did you disappear to?" Mike opened the door and climbed in. "Since you're sitting behind the wheel, I assume you're planning to drive back. Why did you leave so suddenly? We could have gotten a few more shots of His Royal Sheikhness mingling with the hoi polloi."

"Right." Chloe gunned the engine and shot out of the press parking area. "I took plenty of shots. The paper's only going to use one or two. I think the handshake came out great. Shows solidarity in our relationship with—"

"Stop it, McDonald. What's the scoop?"

"Nothing. I got what I came for. The crowd was starting to get to me. Drop it, okay?"

"Sure. Glad you're driving. I can read more of his background since I still don't have a special angle to use."

He reached for the folder in the middle of the seat and began reading the biographical information Paul collected.

"This guy's been around. Schooling in England and the U.S. Set up foreign offices for some of their state-run businesses. Seems to prefer England and France to the other European countries, though he visits Switzerland a lot in the winter." He hummed tunelessly as he continued to read.

"Sure likes the ladies. Was close to a couple of English ladies--ummm, Lady Susan Fairchild--fancy. A French actress. Married a few years back."

Chloe's hands gripped the wheel tightly as everything started to spin. For a moment tears threatened. She took a deep breath, swallowing the ache in her throat. Why shouldn't he have married? Just because she never planned to permit anyone that close again was no reason for him to abstain.

Obviously the promises he'd made to her had no binding effect. But then, she'd known that for years.

Only, somehow, she'd thought—

"Oh, wife died a couple of years later. No kids, apparently. He's got three brothers, all younger."

The portion of the background material Chloe had read on the ride to the White House had surrounded the trade treaty that was being negotiated. She hadn't read any of the personal stuff. Now she was glad. Could her voice have remained normal?

She was having trouble focusing on her driving. Thankfully the office was just up ahead. She couldn't wait to get to her desk. Even though she shared a large room with a dozen others, the shoulder-high partitions gave a modicum of isolation and privacy.

It was over. She'd seen him and survived.

The rest of the day would be busy enough to keep her thoughts off the man.

Tomorrow was Saturday, nothing scheduled for her. Maybe she and Mackenzie could go on a picnic in Rock Creek Park or visit that video store in Alexandria that specialized in old horror films. For some unfathomable reason, Mackenzie loved old movies of that type.

The important thing was that Chloe would go on with her life. A thread from the past had briefly touched her, but nothing had changed.

Chloe took another deep breath and tuned out Mike's muttering, focusing on getting her emotions under control.

Two

The brief cool spell from Thursday's rain ended Friday afternoon. Saturday dawned hot and muggy. By midmorning Chloe wished for the thousandth time that she had a place in the mountains. It'd be cooler there. The house was air-conditioned, but she had yard work to do and a dirty car to wash.

Mackenzie had spent the night at her friend Stephanie's and wouldn't be home until later.

Chloe needed to keep busy. She'd finish her chores, then be free to spend the afternoon with her daughter. She had to stop thinking about yesterday's press conference and the unexpected assignment with Karif.

Had he really recognized her? Or had it been too long since he'd seen her?

Had she been only one in a long line of women? From what Mike had muttered, the sheikh was used to escorting beautiful and prominent women in several countries.

While not exactly a flamboyant playboy, he obviously would have no time for a quiet photojournalist he'd once known briefly a decade before.

Chloe finished mowing the lawn and put the mower away in her detached garage. She glanced at the street when the sleek black limousine purred to a stop in front of her house. She stood in the driveway, her heart sinking. Transfixed, she watched as the car stopped and a man climbed out of the front and reached back to open the rear door.

Transfixed, she stared.

Sheikh Karif bin Shakirah climbed out and stood on the sidewalk, surveying her house through dark glasses. She couldn't determine from his expression what he thought, but it really didn't mattered. For one brief moment she toyed with the idea of dashing back into the garage and hiding.

But it was too late. He'd seen her.

He strode confidently toward her.

Chloe couldn't move. She stood where she was and idly wondered where his robes were. He was dressed in a business suit as normal as any American businessman. He was as tall as she remembered. He'd already been a man when she'd known him, but now she was seeing him with different eyes.

Her heartbeat increased. She wished she'd had a chance to shower. She had bits of grass clinging to her legs and she felt hot and sweaty.

Totally not ready to face him. Whatever would she say?

Karif's scanned Chloe as he slowly walked across her lawn, She looked almost as young as when he'd last seen her, yet she had to be twenty-nine by now. She'd be thirty on her next birthday. Hard to believe. He still remembered her as the wide-eye young college student so enthusiastic about so many things.

He smiled as he let his gaze trail down the length of her. She wore short white shorts, almost indecently skimpy. Attire like that was suited only for the beach in his country. These revealed a long length of tanned legs dotted with grass. The shorts fit like a second skin. For a moment he wished she would turn so he could see how they hugged her bottom.

The yellow tank top she wore enhanced the honey tone of her skin. Her light brown hair was much shorter than when he'd known her. Yet the mop of curls that danced around her face was enchanting.

His smile faded when he drew close enough to see the wary, unfriendly expression in her brown eyes.

"Hello, Chloe," he said. He wished he'd changed out of the suit before coming. But he'd been too impatient to see her again. He'd left immediately after the breakfast meeting concluded.

Now he felt too warm, too over dressed. And her revealing casual attire didn't help his temperature one bit.

"Do I bow or curtsy?" she asked. She stood tall, feet spread, her chin tilted a bit pugnaciously, her gaze hostile.

He smiled grimly. Some things hadn't changed. She always had a smart remark ready. He had an almost overwhelming urge to lean over and kiss her until she was breathless.

"Neither. A simple 'Hi, it's been a long time,' would do."

"It has been a long time. If I had known you were coming by, I would have read up on proper etiquette. Or left home at first light."

"Chloe."

She looked beyond him at the limousine. "Sorry I don't have servants' quarters where your chauffeur and bodyguard can wait." She looked him square in the face. "How long are you staying?"

"If you'd care to invite me inside, I'd appreciate it. It's hot out here and I'm not exactly dressed for the weather."

"It must be as hot in your country. The one you never talked about. The one you never told me about when we knew each other in Berkeley."

She blinked, annoyed at the prick of angry tears behind her lids. Her hands clenched into fists as the outrage spread.

He raised an eyebrow, his gaze never leaving hers.

"It is as hot in my country but I live beside the Mediterranean. It's pleasant there. We often have a breeze, which keeps the temperature manageable."

He glanced around the neighborhood. The houses were built fairly close together, the yards nicely maintained. It was an older neighborhood, the trees mature and lush. The shrubbery surrounding her house needed a trim. The grass was freshly cut.

"Yes, well, I'm not quite dressed for such illustrious company. And I'm sure my house would not—"

"Chloe, shut up." He whipped off the sunglasses and stared down into her astonished gaze. "It took most of yesterday and part of today to locate you. Why didn't you come to see me after the ceremonies? You must have recognized me. I certainly recognized you the instant I saw you."

"I never thought about it," she lied. "I'm surprised you bothered to look me up. I thought you made it quite clear ten years ago that our *friendship* ended."

"And you didn't hang around very long to find out, did you? I thought you'd planned to finish your education at the university."

"Plans change all the time. You should know that as well as the next man. Of course, I was the only one planning a marriage, you were planning an escape."

"I can explain my part of what happened, but I've often wondered at yours."

"There was no 'my part' in your leaving. And at least you knew who I was. I don't even know what to call you. Is it 'Your Highness'?"

Karif reached out to brush an errant curl from her cheek, giving in to the impossibly strong urge to touch her, however briefly. "You used to call me Karif." His hand dropped to his side, his fingers still tingling with heat from her satin soft skin.

Run! Chloe fought the command her mind was sending.

If she had an ounce of sense, she would run from this man as far and as fast as she could. He'd hurt her unbearably. She didn't need the confusion and turmoil his presence brought. She shivered at his touch. The feel of his fingers on her cheek instantly evoked memories of years ago.

His eyes were so dark and deep she felt she was drowning. He should have kept on the glasses. She felt safer with that slight barrier. Now she couldn't pull her gaze from his.

She felt flushed with heat and it wasn't from the sun. *Where have you been all this time,* she wanted to shout.

What have you done? Why did you betray me with lying words of love and then vanish?

Taking a deep breath, Chloe caught the scent of his aftershave, deep and dark and mysterious, just like the man. Mixed with the fragrance of the fresh-cut grass it was earthy and entirely too enticing. Her anger deepened-- some of it turned on herself for feeling anything beyond the fury of betrayal.

"Chloe, ask me inside," he insisted.

She closed her eyes at the inevitable and nodded, turning to lead the way. She'd visit for a minute. Then he'd be on his way.

Tilting her head, she threw back her shoulders. He was a dignitary visiting her country. It no longer mattered that he was also the man who'd broken her heart. She'd be gracious, formal and distant.

Chloe stopped suddenly. *Mackenzie would be coming home soon.*

She had to get their talk over with quickly. She couldn't have Mackenzie arrive while Karif was here.

The old anger she felt was instantly overshadowed by concern. She didn't want Karif to find out about Mackenzie.

"This really isn't a good time," Chloe said a bit desperately. She didn't want them to go into the house. Didn't want him to stay another minute. Mackenzie could be home any second. Her glance flickered down the sidewalk. Stephanie only lived a block away.

"I'm only going to stay a few minutes. I finished one set of meetings this morning and will need to review my notes before getting ready for another one at lunch. Then there's a reception tonight. But I wanted to see you first."

"Why?"

"Chloe, move." He reached out to take her upper arm in his hand, propelling her gently along.

He continued up the walk to her front door, his hand like a hot band around her arm, sending shimmering waves of longing and forgotten desire .

Involuntarily, Chloe brought her arm in close. Big mistake. Sparks ignited a flame deep within. She pulled away, forcing him to release her. He had walked out on her ten years ago. He was only here today because of a chance encounter on the White House lawn.

If Paul's baby hadn't decided to be born yesterday, Karif would never have seen her, would never have felt whatever obligation or curiosity had driven him to show up today.

And she wouldn't be torn apart by her own emotions. She'd resist wanting to find out every scrap of information about him. She needed to protect herself from becoming involved.

How dare he show up as if he was a long-lost friend. She longed to yell at him for the past, yet despite everything, she felt a tug of familiar physical attraction. She needed to guard her heart wisely. He was here for a short time, and then gone again. Never forget!

Chloe opened the door and stood aside as he entered. Curious to see his reaction to her home, she studied him as he stepped into the living room and surveyed it.

"Nice. It reminds me of your apartment in Berkeley." He strode into the center of the room as if he owned the place. Blatantly masculine in his appraisal, he looked at her furnishings and the collections of photographs she'd taken now hanging on the wall.

"Have a seat," Chloe said talking quickly before he noticed the personal photos lining the mantle. Conscious of the minutes ticking by, she needed to end the meeting as quickly as possible.

Karif sat on the sofa, watching her closely as she crossed to a nearby chair.

He'd scarcely aged at all, she thought as she stared at him, waiting to hear what he had to say. Wishing things had been so different.

His hair was rich and glossy black, not a trace of silver showing. His skin was smooth and tanned, except for the lines near his eyes. His shoulders seemed broader than she remembered. But maybe it was the suit, it looked as if it had been designed specifically for him, which it probably had.

He was a sheikh, remember, well able to afford the best.

"You are looking well." His eyes traveled over her again, lingering on the soft swell of her breasts clearly defined by her damp cotton top, then moving slowly down her long tanned legs.

"What do you want?" she said curtly, longing to snatch a coat from the closet to cover herself. She was disturbed by the tingling awareness that shimmered through her at his look. The skin on her arm was still blazing from the feel of his hand.

She glared at him, willing him to say his piece and leave.

He looked totally out of place in her modest living

room. He was better suited to elegant continental drawing rooms or royal palaces or the endless expanse of Arabian deserts. Certainly not a small space like her home.

"I wanted to explain what happened ten years ago," he said. "I know my leaving was, shall we say, unexpected. Unforeseen. I tried to contact you later but you'd moved and no one knew where." His tone was cool, almost impersonal.

"Oh? Yes, I moved. There were...I...moved." She swallowed. What could she say? It made no difference now. And at the time, she'd had no choice.

This wasn't about her. It had been Karif who walked away without a backward glance.

"Why did you try to reach me?" she asked to fill the silence that stretched between them.

Chloe sat on the edge of the chair, unable to relax. She hadn't known he'd tried to reach her. If she'd been able to stay longer in Berkeley, would things have turned out differently?

Probably not.

She wiped nervous palms against her shorts.

"To let you know where I was, of course."

"I see," she said politely. She wanted him gone. Couldn't he tell? His very presence reminded her of a time she wished to forget.

"Damn, I don't want some polite little response, Chloe. Didn't you care that I had left so abruptly?"

"Of course I did." She held her breath for a moment, but the old anguish wouldn't be stilled. "I thought we were in love," she said, almost yelling with the old anger and hurt. "I thought we were going to be married and share our lives together. Instead, you disappeared without a word. Then I find out ten years later that you're not even the man I thought I knew—"

"Hey, Mom, did you see that cool car in the front? Is it a limo? Who—"

Mackenzie paused in the archway to the living room when she spotted her mother and the stranger. The man rose and turned to face her. For an endless moment, time stood still.

Oh, man, not this, too. Chloe couldn't bear it.

She stared at her daughter, examining every feature, trying to see her as Karif would see her. Mackenzie was an average American girl, dark eyes, light brown hair, childish features.

Please, don't let him guess.

Three

Karif felt as if someone had kicked him in the gut. Chloe had a child!

Her short curly hair was light brown with sun-bleached highlights. Her eyes were unexpectedly dark and wide-spaced. Except for the eyes this child was the spitting image of Chloe.

Karif stared at the little girl. Anger flared as the evidence of her lack of faithfulness stared back at him. He'd been a fool to think she'd wait for him. Had their relationship been only a brief college fling?

Had she turned to someone else the minute he'd disappeared? By the child's apparent age, she must have.

"The limo is mine," he said to the little girl. "Would you like to see it?" He needed a few minutes. The hot throb of rage that filled him needed to be calmed before he spoke to her again.

"Would I? That'd be great. Mom, have you seen it?" Mackenzie smiled and came into the room, dropping her sleeping bag and backpack on the floor and dancing over to her mother.

Chloe reached out and ruffled her daughter's hair, smiling with difficulty. The last thing she wanted was this.

Could she bluff her way through?

"I've not seen that particular one, but I've ridden in one before. If it's all right with--" She couldn't even call him by name. "It's fine with me. But don't get it dirty."

"Oh, Mom, Stephie and I were swimming. I'm squeaky clean."

Mackenzie smiled at the stranger and dashed to the door. Pausing, she looked back. "Will the driver let me see it?"

"I'll make sure." Karif crossed the room and followed her outside.

Chloe watched as the two left, a feeling of imminent catastrophe claiming her. She felt paralyzed, mesmerized by the turn of fate she had no control over. Karif had to realize. The age was right. She wasn't married, did he know that?

What would she do if he realized Mackenzie was his?

More important what would *he* do?

She observed them through the front window for a little while then went into the kitchen and took three glasses from the cupboard. She wondered how long it took to examine a limousine.

Time passed slowly as she prepare lemonade. How long was *he* staying? Nervously she hunted for a tray. Normally she and Mackenzie each got their own drinks. Today she'd be a bit more formal. The circumstances seemed to call for it. Besides, it gave her something to do.

"How old is your daughter?" Karif stood in the doorway. His expression was hard, remote. His eyes stared at her like black ice.

Chloe turned to face him. She wasn't the one who had

done anything wrong. He was the one who had left her without a word.

"I beg your pardon?"

"Dammit, Chloe, don't play games with me. How old is your daughter? How long did you wait before finding another man?"

Chloe blinked and looked away lest he guess how surprised she was at his belief.

He didn't know Mackenzie was his!

She took a deep breath. "Actually, I don't believe that's any of your business," she said.

The words were scarcely out of her mouth before he crossed the room in two furious strides and grabbed her arms. Leaning over until his face almost touched hers, his dark eyes blazed down into hers, he ground out, "As you so conveniently remembered in the other room, we were supposed to have been in love. I tried to contact you less than a month after leaving Berkeley and you were already gone. Had you connected up with someone in that short a time?"

"Let go! How dare you come into my life again and talk about what we had ten years ago! You're the one who lied about his identity, kept his background a secret. What kind of relationship did we have when you weren't even honest enough to tell me your full name? It was nothing but lies. From start to finish—"

"It was not lies. Not all of it. Give me strength, you try a man's patience. I came today to explain but find that I needn't have bothered. Obviously you didn't miss me long enough to matter."

He let her go and turned, getting his emotions under

control.

Chloe leaned against the counter, her knees trembling so much she was afraid they wouldn't hold her.

"Oh, that's just great try to make me look like the one who did wrong. What about you? I called and got no answer. I was so worried about you. I went to your apartment and begged the landlord to let me in. He knew we'd been close. How do you think I felt when I saw the empty apartment? Not one stitch of clothing remained. Not one book. Nothing. You vanished without a trace and without a single word to me."

She remembered how devastated she'd felt.

"Would it have hurt to drop me a postcard or call from the airport to say you were leaving? I thought you were in trouble. After not hearing from you all these years, I thought that you were dead! I never even knew your full name or where you were from. I never knew you were a sheikh!"

She hadn't meant to raise her voice. But the accusation was too much. The old anger bubbled up and spewed forth.

"Chloe."

"Don't start with me, Sheikh Karif bin Shakirah. You mean nothing to me now. Where have you been for the last ten years? Playing Rudolph Valentino, sheikh of the desert?"

She shouldn't have said that. Couldn't she keep her mouth shut? Now he'd think—

She didn't care what he thought. She just wanted him to leave, to give her a chance to get her life back the way it was before Friday morning. She didn't like feeling so out of control. She didn't want to churn up old memories, old regrets.

He glared at her, his manner intimidating as he drew himself up to his full height, almost threatening.

"I came here today to tell you what happened, why I left so suddenly. I thought we could see each other while I was in the States, see—"

"See if we could take up where we left off while you're here? What did you expect me to be, your Washington paramour? No thanks, I'm busy."

His gaze locked with hers. "You're correct, you didn't know where to find me. And I couldn't find you. I tried."

"You left the end of May. I couldn't stay once school was out. You didn't try soon enough. A phone call, that's all it would have taken. You knew my number, you called it often enough. One lousy phone call. You said you loved me, you knew I loved you! One phone call, a note, *something.* After all we'd meant to each other, surely I deserved something better than what I got."

She shut her mouth. All the anger and anguish of that long-ago time was threatening to overwhelm her. She took a deep breath, fighting for control.

It was in the past. She had made something of her life as a single parent and she sure didn't need him barging in on her life at this late stage. Especially when his staying record was so poor.

"There were circumstances…"

He glanced at his watch, frowning. "Never mind, it's more than I can go into right now. I'm already late. You get your wish. I have to leave. But we're not through. Tomorrow I haven't any appointments until a reception at seven. I can come by—"

"We have nothing to discuss. Just go." She couldn't deal with this again.

"I beg to differ. I want to talk to you about what happened ten years ago. And I want to hear about your daughter."

His voice was hard, the look he gave her determined and implacable.

She shook her head, but he stepped closer, reaching for her shoulders. His hands were warm. His touch sent sizzling tingles through her that she longed to deny it. She was still so blasted angry she thought she'd explode.

"Yes, Chloe, tomorrow we'll talk."

"Not here, then. Not with Mackenzie around."

Was there anything he could say to make any sense after all this time?

Mackenzie was his child. Perhaps she owed it to him to at least tell him something about her.

But that was as far as she was willing to go. She refused to let him know Mackenzie was his. She and Mackenzie had their lives and he obviously had his.

A very different life than she'd ever envisioned over the years.

She'd been a fool to waste one minute of worry on him. He lied to her, made love to her, then abandoned her for the luxurious life approaching royalty, while she'd been so afraid he'd been in trouble.

His thumb traced the line of her collarbone. Chloe reached to grab his wrists, tug his hands away from her. She couldn't think when he was touching her. He was too potent. His dark eyes too mesmerizing for coherent thought, his warm skin too tempting. She needed space.

"Just what are you suggesting?" she said.

"That's part of what we'll need to discuss. Tomorrow."

"Not here," she repeated, feeling uncertain.

"I'll send the limo for you. We can talk at my hotel."

She shook her head. "I don't know."

She didn't want to go there, on his own turf, so to speak. Yet she dare not risk Mackenzie's overhearing them.

A grim smile crossed his lips. "I do."

It was almost an order--yet with his smile the dimple deepened and Chloe's heart fluttered. Her fingertips actually ached to touch him, to feel his warmth, dip into that slight indentation. Her eyes drank him in.

He was so gorgeous, more so now than ten years ago. Her heart thumped heavily at the very sight of him. She longed to turn the clock back a decade. Longed for an endless moment to rediscover the love she'd once known.

Wished she did not know it had all been built on lies and deceit.

"I'll send the car at one, then we'll talk."

She hesitated, catching her bottom lip between her teeth, knowing the uncertainty must show in her expression.

How could she guarantee this wasn't leading to further disaster?

He tipped her chin up with a long, tanned finger, and gazed down into her light brown eyes, his narrowed as he looked at her.

She swallowed hard, feeling his soft breath caress her

cheeks, feeling his heat and strength through his finger.

Could he read her mind? Could he feel the anger that still simmered below the surface, see the hesitation in her gaze?

Slowly, he lowered his face until his lips brushed against hers. Once, twice, he skimmed across hers, then withdrew. "Tomorrow at one."

With that he was gone. Chloe stared after him, listening to his quick stride down the hall, to the sound of the front door opening and closing. Then the silence.

Blood coursed through her veins, pounding in her ears, scorching every inch of her. She rubbed her tongue lightly across her lips, tasting him, feeling the imprint of his lips as clearly as if he were still present.

Turning to the sink, she ran cold water, splashing it on her face, rubbing her lips to erase his touch.

She wasn't some starry-eyed teenager. She was too smart and too scarred to ever fall victim to his charm again. She'd learned that lesson well.

The front door slammed. Mackenzie hurried into the kitchen, her face radiant with happiness.

"Oh, Mom, that limo was so cool! It was almost as big as my bedroom. And it has a TV and a refrigerator. Not a big one like ours but a little one. And there was soda. Fahim, that's the driver, said I could have one, but I didn't want to spill it. The inside had carpet all over the floor. It was so cool."

Chloe smiled at her daughter, her heart catching again at the sight of her. She'd lived with her baby for more than nine years, but somehow, after seeing Karif today, she realized anew what a treasure her daughter was.

Reaching out, she drew the little girl into a warm hug, hoping nothing would ever change for them.

Afraid everything was changing.

Four

"So you thought that was pretty cool, huh? What's really fun is to ride in one and imagine you're a princess or something and wave to the other cars on the road. Because of the tinted windows, no one can see in, so you can have a fine time pretending."

"Is that what you did when you rode in one?" Mackenzie asked, grinning up at her mother.

"Once. I had a lift to the airport and I was all alone. The window was closed between me and the driver."

Chloe shook her head, how foolish she'd been, but it'd been fun fantasy.

"I wish I were a princess and could ride in a limo every day."

As Mackenzie pulled away and reached for one of the glasses of lemonade, Chloe was struck by the thought that her daughter probably would have been almost a princess if she and Karif had married.

At least in his country.

Had things been different, Mackenzie might have gotten her wish.

Time to change the subject before Mackenzie got caught up in the fantasy--and before Chloe began to doubt the wisdom of keeping Mackenzie's parentage a secret.

"I have a meeting tomorrow afternoon. Do you think you could go to Stephanie's? I'll call her mother to see if it's all right with her. If not, we can ask Mrs. Hanson to come over."

"Sure, that'd be cool. We can swim. I wish we had a pool. It's been so hot lately." Mackenzie pushed out a chair and sat down, turning her glass around and around before her on the table, her eyes on the condensation and the patterns she was drawing through it with her finger.

"You get to swim almost every day at Stephanie's. And I'm glad it's her father that's taking care of the pool and not me."

Mackenzie grinned and nodded. Drinking the last of the lemonade, she set the glass carefully back.

Darting a curious look at her mother, she said carefully, "Mom, who was that man?"

Collapsing on one of the wooden chairs opposite Mackenzie, she looked at her daughter. She didn't have a clue what to say.

"Why do you ask?" she said, stalling for time. Afraid to say the wrong thing, praying for some inspiration, she ran through a dozen possible responses.

"Just wondered. He doesn't talk like us and I never saw him at your office." Mackenzie met her gaze with open curiosity.

Chloe cleared her throat. "He's someone I knew a long time ago. He came to Washington on business and met with the president. I covered the event for the paper and he saw me. So he came to visit."

"Is he nice, Mom? He seems nice, letting me see the limo and all. Or was that just to get rid of me?" Mackenzie wandered over beside her mother, leaning against her when Chloe put her arm around her daughter's small waist.

"I'm sure he wanted you to see the limo. He probably knows what a novelty having one in our neighborhood is."

"That limo was so cool," she repeated. "If he comes to visit again, maybe I can ride in it."

"Don't count on it, toots. He doesn't live in the U.S., you know."

Mackenzie nodded wisely. "That's why he had that funny accent."

"He hardly has an accent at all, merely a charming British intonation."

Charming and sexy. Especially in the dark of midnight when whispering love words. Had she ever forgotten?

"Um, what's for dinner?" Mackenzie asked.

Chloe gave Mackenzie a quick hug then swatted her lightly on the bottom, glad to change the subject.

"We're having deluxe hamburgers on the grill, if you'll help me keep the marauding insects at bay."

Feigning a lighthearted attitude she didn't feel in the slightest, Chloe rose. There were hours yet until dinnertime. She still had the weeding to do in the yard.

Once again, Karif's touch in her life had been brief. She needed to make sure she kept it in perspective.

She wasn't going to dwell on the past. She was firmly entrenched in the present and that's where she was staying. What she and Karif shared had been a fleeting moment. She had her life and he had his, and they were totally different.

The short drive to Karif's hotel the next afternoon was accomplished in total silence. From the time the handsome driver knocked on her door, until she walked into the opulent lobby of the Williams Hotel, Chloe said not a word.

Once ensconced in the luxurious back seat of the limo, she questioned her actions. She should have firmly refused to see him again.

She stared out the tinted windows on the ride. In times past, Karif would have come for her himself, not sent a car.

He'd changed. Of course--he wasn't the Karif she'd known.

Chloe took a deep breath. Older and a lot wiser, she'd deal with the situation. No matter how angry she grew, she'd conduct herself calmly and rationally at this meeting.

Then bid him a cool farewell.

She hoped.

The chauffeur stopped before the portico of the hotel, and quickly opened the door for her. Another man was waiting. He nodded and led the way to the elevator. In seconds they were in the elegant sitting room of the suite.

"Ah, Chloe." Karif stood near the windows as if he had been studying the city of Washington. Today he wore casual clothes, a green polo shirt and tan slacks.

Her eyes flicked over him, then raised to meet his dark gaze. Despite herself, her heart rate increased. He was tanned, from the Mediterranean sun, no doubt, his body strong and lightly muscled.

Holding on to her anger, she stayed near the door, refusing to let herself be charmed by him.

"I'm ready if you wish to tell me about your leaving Berkeley ten years ago."

Long-dormant questions hovered on her lips. The mystery would finally be solved. Then what? Go on with her life as she'd made it.

"It's both simple and complex. Won't you sit down?"

She looked at the facing pair of brocade sofas, glanced warily back at him before slowly crossing to sit on the edge of one.

Karif sat opposite her and faced her across the low Queen Anne table that stood between the sofas.

"I came to America against my father's wishes. He wanted me to continue my education in England, but I was insistent until he reluctantly agreed."

She listened, watching him as he spoke. His eyes never wavered from hers.

"Unexpectedly, my father suffered a major stroke. He'd heard of our--"

He hesitated a moment then continued, "liaison and wanted to end it. To state it bluntly, he used his illness as the means to break us up. Two of the *sajine*, guards for the family, arrived late one afternoon. They were waiting at my apartment when I finished my last final exam. Their orders were to escort me home. I feared my father was dying."

"Was he?" That explained the abrupt departure, but not why she had never heard from him again.

He could have called from the airport or from his home when he arrived.

She also wanted to know why he'd never told her who he was. Why he'd never shared something so basic with her--even after they had become lovers.

"No. He was partially paralyzed, had a mild case of aphasia, speech disorientation. He recovered. But he was very ill for many weeks. We all feared for his life."

"So you stayed to be with him." Chloe understood family loyalty. Of course he'd want to be with his father while the man was so ill.

"I was commanded to do so."

Commanded?" she asked, surprised at the word.

"He was my father. I was commanded to stay to prepare to take his position in the event he died. The stroke gave him the first sting of mortality. He desperately wanted me ready to assume control when he died. My first allegiance was to my father and my family."

"Of course. But you could have let me know! I had the police at your place. I was certain something awful had happened to you. You could have told me where you were, that you were all right. A letter, a call at four in the morning, something!"

For a moment, Chloe relived those frantic days. She'd been so worried and so scared.

"I sent letters but—"

"I never got any. Maybe I'd already left Berkeley before they arrived."

She was restless, nervous.

Rising, she paced to the window, staring blindly out over the view of Washington. She didn't see the marble buildings; she was seeing the past, that frightening time when she'd first realized she was pregnant and alone. Remembering when she'd first accepted that Karif wouldn't be coming back for her.

"I know you never got any. I believe they never left my country."

She spun around. "What?"

"My father had them intercepted. He knew I'd try to contact you. He wanted to end our relationship."

Chloe stared at him, realistic enough to realize a sheikh might have a fling while studying abroad, but that didn't mean he was going to bring the girl home to his family.

So even if he'd remained in Berkeley, they'd never have married. His family would have forbidden it.

How naive of her to assume that love would be enough.

"Well, that's that, then. I'll be going." She turned toward the door, hoping her shaky legs would carry her across the room. She should never have agreed to see him.

Somehow, deep within her, there had been a small bud of hope that something could come of talking over what had happened. That bud died with his words.

"No, don't leave, Chloe. We still have much to discuss."

She paused by the door and turned to face him. For one awful moment, she was afraid she'd blurt out her fury that his family hadn't thought her good enough for him and rail at him for turning aside his daughter so easily.

She bit her lip--he didn't know about his daughter.

And that was how she meant to keep it.

"Come back and sit down," he ordered.

She shook her head. "Maybe in your country you can order people around, but I've got news for you, buster. This is the U.S.A., and we don't take orders from…from sheikhs!"

"I'm not ordering you, Chloe, I'm asking. Please come back and sit down."

Slowly, she returned to the brocade sofa, her eyes glaring into his the entire way.

"There is nothing more to discuss," she said defiantly.

His lips softened into a smile. "But there is, *chérie*, you need to tell me all you've been doing since I last saw you. I've missed you, Chloe. I thought about you for years, wondered where you were, what you were doing. Did you ever marry?"

"Like you did?" she asked.

She'd thought *they* would marry. Instead, Karif had married someone else.

It shouldn't matter, not now, not after all this time. But the fact of the matter was, it did hurt. Intensely.

His face tightened. "My marriage occurred five years after I'd last seen you. At the time, I thought you'd returned my letters and were no longer interested in me. The marriage was an arrangement that my father urged upon me. Don't throw that up into my face, Chloe. It's obvious you wasted no time in finding someone to replace me in your bed."

She felt as if she'd been slapped.

But of course he'd think that. And she had to let him

continue to think that if Mackenzie's identity was to be kept a secret.

"Did you love him?" he asked harshly.

"Who?"

"Mackenzie's father."

She shrugged, her eyes drifting to the left. "I thought I did."

"As much as you loved me?"

Meeting his gaze again, she shook her head. "What we had was nothing. Lies on your part and stupid teenage infatuation on mine."

Ironic that he suspected she'd had another lover. She had never made love to any man but Karif. She hadn't even dated much over the past ten years.

"We talked of marriage," he reminded her.

"Talk is cheap. Where were you when the chips were down?"

"In what way were the chips down?" He went curiously still.

She moved restlessly, avoiding his eyes again. "Never mind. I need to get home."

"Not yet. I'll have Fahim take you back soon. Tell me what led to your job at the *Sentinel.* I thought your major was anthropology."

"Why are you asking? Why do you care?"

"We're different than the two people who knew each other in Berkeley. I want to get to know you again. See who you are now."

"Why?" she repeated.

"When I return to Manasia, I want you to come with me," he said.

She couldn't believe what he'd said. "Why?"

She was beginning to sound like a broken record, yet she could hardly think, much less articulate a full sentence.

"I want you. I wanted you ten years ago, and I want you today." He tossed off the statement as if he were commenting on the weather.

Her heart pounded in her chest, blood rushed through her veins, heating every cell. She wanted to run, to hide, to disappear from his life and never be found again.

"What about your father? Has he changed his mind?"

"That doesn't matter anymore. He died a couple of years ago. I make my own decisions now."

Slowly she shook her head.

"There's time for us to get to know each other again."

"I won't go back with you."

"It's early yet."

Karif crushed his desire to insist. Somehow he'd thought if he just found her, she'd fall into his arms again. He hadn't expected this—and he should have. She was as skittish as a young colt. He was used to gentling horses. Could he apply the same technique to Chloe? Accustomed to instant compliance when giving orders, he realized instinctively that this was different. He'd do better to bide his time and achieve his goal through other means than sheer strength of will.

He had time. He'd use it wisely. Right now, he'd go slowly, seeing if the feelings were still there. Seeing if he could make her fall in love with him again.

"Spend the time I'm in Washington with me. Let's get to know each other as we are now. You're no longer the young college student I once knew. I'm no longer the graduate student so intrigued with all things American," he said.

His tone mocked the young man he'd once been.

"We're too different now. I can't imagine what we'd have in common, what we could talk about." Her eyes watched him warily.

"We never had trouble finding things to talk about before."

It was tempting, oh so tempting.

But Chloe wasn't so naive to think they had a common meeting ground. He was probably rich as Bill Gates while she was a working single mother.

Any time spent with a visiting sheikh would surely give rise to speculation on who she was and why he was seeing her.

She remembered the bio she'd read and the women he'd dated. She didn't want to be another in his long list of women. She couldn't begin to compete with Lady Susan Fairchild or an actress in France.

Shaking her head slowly, she said, "I don't think it's a good idea."

Karif was frustrated. He'd thought she'd be open to resuming their friendship. If not more. Now he needed to draw on patience. If she thought she'd stop him with a simple no, she really didn't know him.

It wouldn't be easy, but nothing worthwhile in life was ever easy.

And after ten long years, he'd found her. The rest would just take a little longer. The most difficult part had already been accomplished.

Five

"Did you know I was planning to go to Berkeley after the meetings concluded here?" he asked.

"No. Why?"

"To look for you."

"What?" She flicked him a startled glance.

"I didn't finish explaining about trying to find you. Actually, after the letters were returned, I tried to contact your father."

"I'm sure that got you nowhere," she said sarcastically.

"It appeared that he didn't want me to contact you any more than my father did. He didn't seem to like me. Is it because I was a foreigner?"

She shook her head. Obviously her father hadn't told Karif why he didn't want anything to do with him. But Chloe knew.

"Did you know my mother's French?" Karif asked.

"Let's face it, Karif, I know very little about you. And what I thought I knew from ten years ago apparently wasn't much."

For one long moment, she wished that she dare trust him as she once had. Wished she could love him again with the soul-soaring intensity of her younger self. Would she ever find such love again?

Would she ever dare to try?

"French is a beautiful language. Especially when making love to a beautiful woman. I have always been glad for my mother's native tongue," he said with his hint of British accent.

She ignored that comment. She remembered him calling her *cherie* when they made love. "How many languages do you speak?"

"Four fluently. We're getting off the topic. Are you deliberately trying to change it?"

"Because your mother's French, your father didn't like your trying to contact me?"

She rubbed her fingertips across the silky brocade. She suddenly wished he sat beside her, instead of across from her. Then she wouldn't be so tempted to let her eyes feast on him. Maybe she could better garner her strength to withstand what was turning out to be an inquisition.

"My parents' marriage wasn't happy. A lot had to do with the cultural differences and the antipathy in my country for the French. My father was determined to make sure I didn't repeat his mistake. So he insisted I marry a woman from my own country. He picked out the bride for me, Sasela. She was the daughter of one of his ministers."

"How long had she been your chosen bride?" Chloe asked.

Karif stared at her with his dark eyes narrowed as if assessing how she'd react to his response. "Since we were teenagers."

Chloe nodded as the chill of the truth penetrated.

"So even when you were in Berkeley you were engaged to her." Her voice was flat, but at least she had hidden the pain his words provoked.

He shrugged. "There was an understanding between our fathers. Sasela and I had only seen each other a few times in our lives. Remember, I spent many years abroad in school."

"All the time you were making love to me, you were engaged to another woman?"

"Not exactly. You're distorting the situation. There was an understanding between our fathers, nothing between Sasela and me."

"Until you married."

"Five years later. You're in no position to judge. How long after I left did you take up with Mackenzie's father?"

Chloe clamped her lips tightly to keep the truth from bursting out. Resentfully, she glared at him. "Can I go home now?"

"Stay for dinner."

"No."

"Stay for dinner," he insisted.

"I can't. You forget I have a daughter. I have to go home to Mackenzie."

"I can't forget that for a moment."

The deep anger that swept through him was startling. He knew Chloe had every right to go on with her life after his father had forced him to return home.

Yet the fact that she had, and so quickly, burned deep. The only saving grace was that Chloe was alone again. He wouldn't let history repeat itself. This time he'd make sure of it. He wanted to see if they had a chance.

"I'll send for your daughter. She can eat with us."

"No!"

Chloe didn't want them around each other. Karif was too astute to remain ignorant of the truth for long if he spent any time with Mackenzie.

He stared at her thoughtfully. "Why not?"

Was there a reason she didn't want her daughter around him? Would the child speak of her father? Did Chloe still have some sort of relationship with the man that she was trying to hide?

Chloe panicked. He was probing too close for comfort. She wanted to escape.

Rising, she took a deep breath and calmly faced him. "I need to go home."

He rose, standing close. She tipped her head back to see him. His dark eyes were as compelling as ever. His masculine scent sent tendrils of awareness shooting through her. She longed to step back but didn't want to give even a hint of her own vulnerability.

He reached out and captured one of her curls between his finger and thumb, brushing over it lightly, the satiny strands as soft as down.

"Why did you cut your hair? I remember it as soft, shiny, so sensuous. I loved it when we kissed and I could gather its fullness in my hands. I always felt as if I held liquid silk in my palms. When we made love, I reveled in the feel of it against my bare skin. When you snuggled against me afterward, I would spread it across my chest and rub its softness against me."

She closed her eyes, almost melting in a puddle of hot

honey. She remembered. Remembered the feel of his fingers smoothing her hair over his chest, threading through the tendrils and massaging her scalp. It had been a special time in the afterglow of love.

She broke away from the spell. She turned and headed to the door, needing to put as much distance as possible between them.

He had the power to produce hot urgent need within her with just a look or a touch. After all that happened she couldn't want anything from him. Taking a deep breath, she tried to get her senses into order.

Karif watched her. She wasn't indifferent to him. Why not see what could develop between them again?

"I cut it because it was too much trouble to keep wearing it long."

She'd never tell him that she'd cut it off because she remembered every touch he'd ever given her and had wanted to change things drastically enough to forget some of the torment of her life without him.

"I'm glad no other man enjoyed your long hair. I like knowing I was the only one to spread it across my chest," he said softly.

She whipped around to face him, hands on her hips. "It's my hair and I can wear it however I like. It's none of your business how many men —"

His dark eyes blazed back at her.

"'And how many men have you had over the years?" His voice was as smooth as cream, but the dark gleam in his eyes was pure danger.

She blinked and tilted her chin. "Not many," she confessed. "Not nearly as many men as women you've had, if the reports my colleague Mike read to me are anything to go by."

"How many?" he asked again.

Her eyes dropped to his lips, drawn into a firm line as he waited for the answer. She shifted to look at the spot on his cheek where the dimple appeared when he smiled. She wanted to lie, wanted to pretend she'd had dozens of lovers, that she was a swinging woman who hadn't lived the life of a woman scared to trust her own emotions, her own judgment.

But she couldn't.

"None of your business," she whispered. She opened the door.

"I'll have Fahim to take you home." He stepped to the phone.

In only moments she was on her way.

Karif watched from the window as she left, wishing she'd asked him to go with her.

But he didn't want to see her home again. Didn't want to see the signs of her life without him.

At one time he'd planned to face his family's disapproval and risk everything for her.

He was glad now he had not. He'd see her while he was in Washington, invite her to Manasia for a visit. If they didn't fall in love again, he'd go on as he had before. Maybe marry again. While his brothers all had children, he had none. It was time to establish a family.

Salid entered quietly. "Is there anything you wish, Excellency?"

Karif turned from the window.

"Yes. The woman who was just here, Chloe

McDonald, has a child. A little girl. Find out when she was born, where and who the father is. A copy of the birth certificate should provide all that. Then send a large bouquet of flowers to her. At her office, I think."

"Very good." Salid left as quietly as he had entered.

Karif frowned, annoyed at his obsession at learning more about the man who'd fathered Mackenzie but determined to find out what he could.

He wanted to know everything about Chloe--all she'd done since he'd last seen her.

It was after five when Chloe reached home. She was tired. The events of the day had bombarded her nonstop. First, the worry about seeing Karif, then the confrontation with him. To top it off, the fear he'd find out about Mackenzie almost made her frantic.

She headed for the phone. It was time Mackenzie came home. Tomorrow she'd invite Stephie over for dinner. Chloe wanted to give the Andersons a break from her daughter practically living at their house.

Right now, she just wanted to see Mackenzie, be with her.

"Hi, Margie? It's Chloe. I'm back, you can send the ragamuffin home. I appreciate your taking care of her."

"She's never any trouble. She and Stephie swam, then we rented some movies and they've been giggling together like maniacs. Sure you don't want us to keep her a little longer?"

"Thanks, but no. Send her home. Thanks again. Maybe Stephie can come over for dinner tomorrow?"

"Sounds great. I'll let Sam know we can plan a dinner for two."

Chloe went to the front door, impatient to see her daughter, to hold her safely in her arms.

Talking with Karif had been harrowing.

She was annoyed she still felt some attraction toward him, especially after all she'd learned this afternoon.

But there it was. Her best bet was to stay far away from him. He'd be gone soon. And she'd make sure she knew if he were ever returning to Washington so she could arrange to be gone.

The flowers arrived the next morning at the *Sentinel* office while Chloe was out on assignment. She learned about them the instant she stepped onto the floor.

"Wow, Chloe, wait until you see what you got," Lana the receptionist said with a broad smile.

"Chloe, who are the flowers from?" a colleague called as she passed his cubicle.

"Hey, love, who are you seeing that owns a florist shop?" another called, rocked back in his chair.

The comments followed her to her desk. There sat the most beautiful bouquet she'd ever seen. The spring flowers were fresh and colorful. She recognized the daisies, roses and carnations. Some of the more exotic blossoms were unknown to her. But the arrangement was lovely. And lavish.

Her fellow journalists and copy editors crowded around, asking who the flowers were from, urging her to open the note that sat so prominently among the blooms.

She shrugged off her camera case and reached for the envelope, a feeling of dread starting. Glancing up, she spotted Mike watching her. For one long second, she hoped the flowers were from him. It would be so much easier to deal with. But she had a strong feeling they weren't.

Have dinner with me. Karif.

She schooled her features to remain calm. She couldn't give way to frustration and nerves in front of her coworkers. Slipping the note back into the envelope, she tossed it carelessly on her desk. Pinning on a bright smile, she faced the group.

"Flowers from a friend."

"A rich friend," someone murmured.

"You act as if you've never seen flowers before," she protested.

"Not sent to you."

She nodded, acknowledging the fact. "They're pretty, aren't they?" She had to keep it light.

Obviously seeing they'd get no more out of her, the others began drifting back to their desks until only Mike remained.

He crossed over and glanced at the small, white envelope, then looked at her with narrowed eyes.

"Something you want to tell your partner?" he asked softly.

She stepped away, irritated.

"No. As I told everyone they're from a friend. Sheila's right, I've never had flowers sent to me before." She shrugged. "First time for everything, I guess."

For a moment, she allowed the pure delight at the gesture to rush through her. Then practicality reared up. "But I'll have to make it clear he's not to do anything like this again. I don't want talk about it."

"Honey, you've got talk around this place for the next few days. Give in and tell a couple of friends as much as you dare. That will keep the rest from badgering you. By the way, I've got a lead on a story about a drug bust going down, want to ride along in case it pans out?"

"Sure." Tucking the card into her camera case, she took another look at the beautiful bouquet before following Mike out.

She'd have to speak to Karif about sending her flowers. Let him know he couldn't do it again. It caused talk and that was the last thing she needed.

When Chloe turned onto her street that evening her heart dropped when she saw the long limo parked in front of her house. Her nerves stretched taut, she turned into her driveway then hurried from her car to the house. How long had he been here?

She stopped in the archway to the living room. Mrs. Hanson, Mackenzie's baby-sitter and neighbor, was chatting calmly with Karif. He rose when he heard Chloe and watched her as she looked at him, at Mrs. Hanson, then looked around the room.

"I didn't know you were coming by," she said breathlessly.

"I invited you for dinner. I called your office and they said you'd received the flowers, so I assumed you'd also accepted the invitation," he said coolly.

She flushed. She'd been in such a hurry to leave the office she'd neglected to call to refuse the dinner invitation.

"I'm sorry, I should have called. I can't go."

Her heart was racing. Where was Mackenzie? Had she spent any time with Karif? What had Mrs. Hanson told him about her daughter?

Karif raised an eyebrow. "Indeed, and why not?"

"I--"

"If you need a sitter, my dear, I'd be happy to stay longer," Mrs. Hanson said genially.

"Or we could take Mackenzie with us," Karif said easily.

Karif watched Chloe closely. The last time he'd suggested such a thing, she'd refused.

"No! I mean, I'm sure the kind of places you're used to dining in wouldn't be suitable for a child. They get very restless, you know."

He remained silent while she spoke with her baby-sitter.

"I do have other plans for tonight, Mrs. Hanson, but thank you for offering to stay. Is Mackenzie home?"

"She and Stephanie are just finishing their homework in Mackenzie's room." Mrs. Hanson began gathering her things. "If you don't need me, I'll go on home now. I didn't start anything for dinner, you didn't leave a note."

"No, I plan to take the girls out to dinner and then maybe go shopping at the mall." Chloe cast a glance at Karif. "I already made plans to go out. I should have called. I'm sorry."

He nodded. "Maybe tomorrow."

She stared at him. What could she say? She didn't want to see him again. She certainly didn't want him coming to her house where he would see Mackenzie. Yet she couldn't keep inventing previous engagements. Especially in front of Mrs. Hanson. She led a very quiet life. What could she come up with that would satisfy him? Wishing for some inspiration, she stared helplessly at him scrambling for an idea.

Karif's lips twitched. She looked absolutely floored. Hadn't she expected him to persevere? If she truly had plans for tonight, which he suspected she did not, he'd try for tomorrow night.

Maybe that would be even better. He had the reception to attend at the Department of State. He'd like to have her attend with him.

"Tomorrow, then. At eight. I have to attend a reception first, then we can have a late dinner."

Six

Chloe stood perfectly still as Karif brushed the back of his fingers against her cheek in farewell, then departed. It had been so long since she'd felt the gentle touch of a man's hand.

She shivered slightly at the thought of tomorrow night.

She should have had things lined up every evening until he went back to his country.

She should have come up with some excuse for tomorrow night. Normally, she could think fast on her feet. Somehow, around Karif, her brain stalled.

Unless she could come up with some compelling reason to refuse, she'd spend hours in his company. Thanks goodness they wouldn't be alone. They'd attend the reception. She would decline a late dinner and insist on returning home. That would end it.

She hoped.

Still tingling from his touch, Chloe stared out of her front window as the limo pulled away. She could scarcely breathe. Karif's touch shimmered through her.

She wanted to give way to the longings that surged through her and throw herself into his arms, beg him to kiss her, demand that he hold her and never let her go.

But that'd never happen. She was awash with old, almost forgotten, feelings. Heat seeped into every cell. Her heart banged heavily. It had been ten years, surely she was over him by now.

For a moment, Chloe let some of the happy memories of their time in Berkeley surface. For so long she'd pushed them away, feeling the anguish of knowing they were memories that would never be repeated. But she and Karif had had such fun. They laughed and shared in their delight in all aspects of college and the freedom of youth.

They'd talked for hours on end, sharing ambitions, planning how best to save the world. Then, near the end of the spring semester, they'd made love. Not often, maybe only three or four times. Not nearly enough to last a lifetime.

But it'd been wonderful, the most amazing experience she'd ever had. She'd felt loved, cherished, adored.

Which had made the pain of his disappearance all the sharper.

For a while she'd touched heaven, only to have it all inexplicably vanish.

Now she knew it would never have ended differently.

She dare not trust her heart or emotions to him again. The knowledge that he'd lied about who he was and the fact that he'd had no intentions of ever going beyond an affair in Berkeley rocked Chloe. She thought she knew him. Obviously, her judgment in such matters was impaired. She felt too uncertain to trust her judgment again.

She never wanted to live through such hurt and anguish a second time.

Karif settled back in the limo as Fahim drove away from Chloe's house. Salid turned to look back from the front seat as if to ask a question, but upon seeing Karif's expression, he remained silent.

Karif clenched a fist displaying some of the anger that swept through him. Chloe could have worked around the children's dinner. Her baby-sitter could have managed the two little girls of that he was certain. He should have challenged her on the matter.

He was striving for patience, but she pushed his limits. The older woman would have watched Chloe's daughter. He and Chloe could have dined quietly, talked of their lives, caught up on what each had done. Taken steps to know each other again.

If she thought he was so easily put off, she really didn't know him. Starting tomorrow with the reception, Chloe would discover he wasn't so easily put off .

His fists relaxed as he thought of how soft and feminine she was. Her skin felt like silk when he'd brushed her cheek.

He craved her now even more than when they'd been in Berkeley. The years had done nothing to reduce the strength of his feelings for her. She was in his blood and no matter what obstacles she threw in their way, he wanted to be with her again.

He hadn't had a choice ten years ago. Now he did.

He wanted to know everything about her--good or

bad. He wanted to know what she'd done after he left. Had she finished college somewhere else? Why was she a photojournalist instead of an anthropologist?

He wanted to know how she liked her job, how she liked living in Washington.

And if she still saw her daughter's father.

He closed his eyes and leaned back in the luxurious cushions. Her stormy eyes danced behind his lids. He smiled. She'd been feisty and passionate when they'd attended Berkeley.

If she thought her anger would deter him, she was crazy. If she only knew how beautiful she was when mad, she wouldn't flare up so easily.

The sparks ignited something deep within him. He wanted to capture that fiery emotion and channel it into something that would burn them both. He'd been denied her love for too long. He couldn't change the past, but he did have some hope for the future. And Chloe definitely fit into that future.

And Mackenzie? He couldn't forget Chloe's daughter.

For a moment he considered the little girl. She was bright and friendly. There was something about her that reminded him of his own mother. His heart ached a little.

Opening his eyes, he gazed unseeing out the window. Despite the circumstances, Chloe had been fortunate. He had no children.

It wasn't too late, of course.

Would she want to have a baby with him? What would such a child be like?

He already had some indication by looking at

Mackenzie. Chloe would raise her children with love and happiness. And he'd devote himself to his children and their mother.

For the remainder of the short journey to the hotel he imagined Chloe pregnant with his child. Imagined how she would look and feel.

Jealousy hit deep and hard. Would the sight of her pregnant with his child erase the images of her with another man?

He hoped so. He didn't want to live with this aching pain forever.

This was ridiculous, Chloe thought the next evening as she peered at herself in the full-length mirror. She'd been to dozens of receptions in Washington during the last few years. There was no reason to be so nervous.

She rubbed her damp palms across her skirt. Yanked her hands away. The dark blue dress was perfect. With a jeweled choker collar, she had no need for any other jewelry. The halter top flowed from the collar to her waist in front, exposing the long length of her spine in the back. The skirt flared and swirled around her legs as she walked. Its short sassy length displayed her long legs to great advantage. The high heels would be fine with Karif; he was tall enough to enable her to wear them.

He also had the ability to make her feel more feminine than anyone else in her life. She wondered if it was a technique mastered in his country or by him alone.

She sighed and studied herself once more. Her makeup was flawless; her hair as good as it got. It didn't help, butterflies danced in her stomach.

The doorbell rang.

Panic flared. She wasn't ready for this--she felt sick. Why hadn't she found an excuse and told him she couldn't go?

Taking a deep breath, she exhaled slowly as she walked to the door and opened it.

"Hello, Chloe." Karif stepped inside and closed the door behind him, his gaze assessing. Reaching out to draw her into his arms, his eyes widened slightly when he realized her dress was backless, but he covered his surprise, drawing her closer and leaning down to kiss her.

She pushed against his shoulder, shortening the embrace.

"I'm ready." It was a lie. She'd never be ready.

"Good." He glanced around. "Someone is watching Mackenzie?"

"She's staying at Mrs. Hanson's for the evening."

He held the door for her while she scooped up her evening bag, a wrap and preceded him from the house. One of his aides held open the rear door to the limo and she slid in, reveling in the sensual feel of the crushed-velvet seat back against her bare skin.

"You're not going to get cold, are you?" Karif asked as he sank into the seat beside her. "There's not much to that dress."

"It's too hot and muggy to get cold. And if this reception is like others I've attended, there will be so many people around, it'll be almost too warm inside." She held up the light wrap. "I have this if I get cold."

"You look beautiful," Karif said as the car pulled

away from the curb.

He wanted to order the driver to take them back to his hotel instead of to the reception. She was as pretty tonight as he had ever seen her and he resented having to share her with anyone. He wanted to hide her away, keep her smiles and laughter directed at him. Her thoughts and attention focused only on him, as she had so strongly focused on him when they had lived in Berkeley. In those days he'd been the most important person in her life.

He wanted that again.

"Thank you," she said in reply to his comment. She glanced over. "You look nice, too," she replied seriously.

He looked good in anything. Or in nothing. Closing her eyes, she turned away, heat seeping into her cheeks. She remembered when they both wore nothing. A deep longing rose. She crushed it ruthlessly.

"Do you know American women are the only ones I know who compliment men on how they look?" he asked whimsically.

"Oh? And have you made a study on this?" she asked. He'd have the perfect research technique, date as many women in as many countries as he could. Not many would turn him down.

His comment reminded her how different their lives were. He was used to dating cosmopolitan women in the world's capital cities. She rarely dated.

They had nothing in common.

After tonight, she'd refuse to see him again. If he even asked.

"Not a measured study as we were taught to do in business classes at Berkeley."

She smiled politely and looked out the window. The evening stretched endlessly.

She shouldn't have come. She was as out of place here as he would be at one of Mackenzie's school plays.

She tried to enjoy the ride. The limousine was a far cry from the old Volkswagen Karif had driven in Berkeley.

For a moment she forgot her anger, forgot his lies and remembered only the fun they'd shared in that old car. Did he ever think about that time? Or had he moved on and not looked back?

The silence became awkward.

Karif broke it. "I'm glad you were able to find a sitter for Mackenzie. Being a single parent must be difficult. Don't you wish to share the burden with someone?"

She shrugged, afraid to answer. She didn't dare let him know how much she'd longed for him the first few years of Mackenzie's life.

"I guess I'm surprised you never married," he said.

"As you did?" She swung around to face him, hurt and anger clashing.

His gaze met hers as he slowly nodded. "As I did. Should I explain about Sasela?"

"Why? We had no commitment between us. You were free-"

He shook his head once, sharply. "No, we had no commitment, but I thought we'd shared love. As I've said, I was unable to locate you after I left. It was important to my father for me to marry, to have children. I am the oldest son. I was almost thirty when I finally gave in to his pressure. Sasela looked a bit like you and I thought she would be enough like you that I would find some measure of happiness."

Chloe stared at him in astonishment. His wife had looked like her? He married Sasela hoping she would be like her?

"And did you find that happiness?" she asked, unable to assimilate all he was telling her.

"Sasela was a loving woman, affectionate and sweet. She tried so hard." He stopped and looked away as if looking into the past. He shook his head. "She wasn't you, Chloe."

"The background reports at the paper mentioned that she died," Chloe said softly, suddenly wishing to offer some comfort, yet not knowing how.

"Yes, a boating accident in the Mediterranean.

"I'm sorry."

"Thank you, I was sorry, too. She was a nice woman."

"And your father didn't push to have you remarry?"

"I think he saw that I was not happy in my marriage and decided to let me find my own way in the future. It also helped that my brothers had each had a son by that time."

The limousine came to a stop at the guard box at the west gate of the White House. A uniformed security guard checked the driver, scanned the car, then permitted them to pass.

"Is this where the reception's being held?" Chloe asked, taking in the sweep of the driveway. She hadn't even thought to ask where the event was taking place.

"No. But we are attending with the president and his wife. We will have a moment with them then go together to the embassy."

"Good grief, Karif, you didn't tell me. I shouldn't be here."

"Why not, don't you like the president?"

"I don't know him. I mean, I've taken pictures of-- Karif, *the president.*"

Karif smiled and reached for her hand, squeezing it lightly.

"He's my official host for this event. It's the last one your government's having for me. I have one more to go to that some oil companies are holding, then I'm finished with official meetings. After that, you and I can spend some time together."

She froze as the limousine drew to a stop. She didn't want to see him again, as she told him. She'd have to deal with that later. For now, the president was heading for their limo.

The night took on a fairy-tale quality. Chloe met the president and his wife and found them friendly and fairly easy to talk to.

She studied the pomp and ceremony surrounding their arrival at the reception, her photographic eye assessing everything as if she were planning a shoot. The bright colors of the evening dresses were a sharp contrast to the dark hues of the men's tuxedos.

Diamonds, rubies and sapphires glittered beneath the crystal chandeliers, throwing flashes of light and rainbow colors through the ballroom.

Despite her protests, she found herself part of the receiving line, next to Karif. It was like a dream--or nightmare. As one person after another looked at her in speculation as they passed down the line, she longed to slink off somewhere and regain some anonymity.

But she kept smiling, shaking hands and responding politely to the friendly comments.

Cameras discreetly caught the line and Chloe was hard pressed not to rush over and snatch them from the photographers. She was used to being behind rather than in front of the lenses. And she hated to think of the inevitable speculation in the paper surrounding her accompanying Karif.

At last they were able to mingle. Karif's hand came to her back, steering her to the first group he wished to speak with. His palm was hot. Its heat swept through her and lighted a blaze deep inside. She leaned slightly against it, knowing she was playing with fire. But for tonight, she'd throw caution to the winds. It was the last time she planned to see him. There was too much past between them to hope their relationship could go anywhere.

"That wasn't so bad, was it?" he asked, leaning closer so she could hear him above the noise.

Looking up, Chloe found his face was mere inches from her own. She licked her lips and spoke softly, "Do you do this kind of thing often?"

The scent of his after-shave teased her nostrils. The heat from his body seemed to envelop her.

Karif watched her. He wanted to kiss her. His eyes found hers and he saw she was aware of the desire that swept through him.

"Only when making official state visits. This is my first in the United States."

If she didn't look so vulnerable and confused, he'd be better able to control his instincts. But he wanted to protect her, cherish her, make sure she never looked lost again.

If not for international diplomacy, he'd find a private corner and kiss her until the fire in his blood cooled.

"Champagne, sir, madam?" A waiter stood before them offering a tray of long-stemmed glasses.

"Thank you." Karif took one, his hand still on Chloe's back. Her skin was so warm, so soft. He never wanted to let go. Slowly his fingertips rubbed the silky texture.

"Yes, thanks." Chloe took a glass and clutched it with both hands. She already felt as if she were floating. Under the circumstances, was drinking a glass of champagne wise?

If Karif didn't stop rubbing her back, she was afraid she would make a fool of herself by throwing her body against his and demanding a million kisses at the very least.

Seven

Twenty minutes later, Chloe was amazed at her acting ability. She was able to talk at some acceptable level, carry on a coherent conversation while her whole being was focused on Karif and his warm caressing fingers, which constantly stroked her bare skin.

And the worst part was she didn't think he even realized what he was doing. He talked with the men and women who came up to him while the entire time his fingertips brushed back and forth.

Yet she didn't have the resolve to move away. This fantasy evening would end soon enough. She wanted the memories to take with her, to have as the long years passed.

When the reception drew to a close, Chloe and Karif again joined the president and first lady in a White House limousine. Too tired to question where Karif's driver was, Chloe climbed in and sat quietly in the spacious seat.

"Where shall we drop you?" the president asked.

"The Williams Hotel. I'll see that Chloe gets home," Karif responded before Chloe could say anything.

When they reached the hotel, she bid their hosts goodnight and entered the lobby with Karif. He headed for the elevator, but Chloe balked.

"I have to get home," she said.

"I planned a late supper for us," he replied, turning to her.

"I can't stay." Refusing to meet his eyes, Chloe looked around the lobby. "I can take a cab."

Karif captured her face in the palms of his hands and tipped it up to meet his gaze. "Stay," he insisted.

She shook her head. "I can't."

"Can't? Or won't?"

She paused for a heartbeat. "I don't want to stay. I went to the reception, now I want to go home."

He studied her for a long moment, then nodded once. Straightening, he released her. "Very well, Fahim can take you home."

"It's awfully late to wake someone up to drive me home. I can catch a cab."

Karif shrugged. "That's Fahim's job. Come up to the suite while I call him. It won't be long."

Chloe hesitated, then reluctantly nodded.

"Did you enjoy tonight at all?" Karif asked as the elevator door slid open. They were the only occupants when the doors closed silently.

"Yes, thank you for inviting me," she said politely.

Karif reached out and drew her into his arms to kiss her. Chloe tried to resist, but the insidious heat began invading her.

When the elevator stopped at his floor, he released her, his hands remaining on her bare shoulder.

"Don't do that again," she said, more furious with her own traitorous reaction than with Karif.

He smiled. "You liked my kisses once.

"That was then."

"And now?" he asked, brushing his thumb across her damp lower lip.

She refused to answer, trying to ignore the heat that sizzled at his touch.

"Will you go with me to the symphony one night this week?" he asked.

Chloe shook her head slowly.

"Chloe, I want to spend time with you while I'm here."

She could hear the frustration in his voice.

"It can't go anywhere, Karif." Her heart was pounding from his kiss. Involuntarily, her gaze found his mouth.

"It can go wherever we want it to go."

"I'll have to see," she stalled. It would be easier to refuse when she didn't feel she was under a spell.

She was afraid, plain afraid to get too close to him. She wasn't able to handle these things casually like other people.

When she loved, it was deep and abiding. She couldn't handle falling for him again only to have him walk away when his visit to Washington ended.

Not that she would let herself fall in love with him again.

Not that he was asking for that. Just a date to the symphony.

He opened the door to his suite and ushered her inside.

"Would you care for a drink?" he asked.

"No. I need to get home."

She held herself stiffly, away from the temptation of being near him. Looking around the living room, she spotted the table set by the window, awaiting to have the food served.

"No need to rush. It's not that late and your daughter is being cared for. Since you won't stay for dinner, stay for a drink."

"I have to work tomorrow. I need to get some sleep." She tried to ignore the pull of the table set for dinner.

"Do you like your job?" Karif asked.

"Very much. I was lucky to find something that I like so well and that pays enough to live comfortably."

"You didn't finish your degree?"

"No. One day I'd like to go back to college, but I don't need a degree to do photography."

Karif reached out to touch her hair lightly, wound a small strand around his finger.

She felt his touch to her toes. Closing her eyes briefly against the longing that invaded, she pulled away.

"Please, could you arrange for me to get home, or I'll call a cab."

His expression grew bleak. "Why is it every time I touch you, you pull away? Does my touch offend you?"

She shook her head. How ironic he thought he offended her.

"Rather the opposite, if you must know," she said, stepping another foot away.

"Opposite?"

"I didn't mean to say that. I need to go."

"Will you dine with me tomorrow?"

"No. I can't."

"Always you can't."

"Try to understand, Karif. I work all day. The evenings are the only time I have to spend with Mackenzie. I want to spend time with her. She's growing up so fast."

"Then I'll take you both to dinner."

"No!" The refusal came instantly.

Karif was silent, studying the nervous woman before him. Slowly, his eyes narrowed. "Is there a reason you don't wish me to see your daughter?"

Chloe swallowed hard and shook her head. "She's just a little girl. I'm sure you'd be bored around her."

"I like children. I have three nephews who I love spending time with. Mackenzie is a bit older and a girl, but I'm sure I wouldn't be bored if we all went to dinner."

She shook her head. She needed to get home. Make sure her little girl was all right.

"How old is Mackenzie, Chloe?" Karif asked softly.

She turned and turned for the door in blind panic. "I have to leave now, Karif. It's late and I need to get home."

She reached for the door, only to find his hand pressing against the wood, holding it closed.

"Chloe."

"Karif, please."

His hand moved to grasp her chin, force her face around to his. "I have Salid researching birth records. He'll come up with Mackenzie's birth certificate. But you can tell me now, how old is Mackenzie?"

"You have no right to her birth certificate!"

"I want to know about her father. I want to know

about the man you turned to after I left." He stared down at her for a long moment.

She stared at him mesmerized, fear choking her throat, her heartbeat rapid, her breath shallow.

"How old is Mackenzie?" he asked, suspicions dawning.

She couldn't speak, couldn't move. She felt frozen.

"How old, Chloe?"

"Nine," she whispered past the block in her throat.

"She's mine, isn't she?" He released her chin to slide his hand around her neck, his thumb on the pulse point at the base of her throat. "Mackenzie's my daughter, isn't she? Isn't she? *Why didn't you tell me?*"

It was too much. The old hurt, the bitterness at his betrayal, the anguish she'd lived through all rushed through her like a tsunami crashing against the shore. Angrily, the words burst forth.

"Just when should I have done that? A week after you walked out without a single word, when I found out I was pregnant? Or sometime in the months that followed? The years that followed? How was I to do that when I didn't know where you were? I didn't even know *who* you were. Mackenzie is *my* daughter. I've taken care of her for nine years. I can take care of her for the next nine. I'm going home."

"Not yet you're not." His hand tightened slightly. "The last thing I expected tonight was to find out I'm a father. You can't just throw that at me and then walk away from it like it was nothing. I want to get to know her. She is *my* daughter."

"Not as far as I'm concerned. I have a daughter, you

have a sheikhdom. I wish us both joy in what we have."
She tried to pull away, but his other hand came up to her
shoulder and he held her.

"You are wrong, Chloe, *we* have a daughter."

Closing her eyes, she hesitated a long moment. The
feel of his hand on her bare skin was intoxicating.
Shimmering streams of awareness flowed through her,
awakening desire that had long lain dormant.

She couldn't cope with all the emotions that churned
inside her—anger, fear, desire. She had to maintain
control, fight for her daughter. Finally, she opened her
eyes, glared at him.

"Let me make one thing clear to you, Karif bin
Shakirah, from the moment I discovered I was pregnant,
until this moment, I have been alone. I carried my baby
alone and I delivered her alone. At night, after working all
day, I walked the floor when she was sick until I was so
exhausted I didn't know how I would make it through the
next morning. But I did. *Alone.* For ten years I've been
alone. Now you waltz in and expect me to welcome you
with open arms. To offer to share my daughter with you
just because you show up? Because you're the sperm
donor? I don't think so! I have a daughter. Leave us
alone!"

Bending over until his nose almost touched hers, he
glared back, his eyes flashing black fire.

"And I have a lonely, empty life, Chloe. I have no
other children. In my family, children are joyfully received
and cherished. I will love my daughter, care for her,
cherish her. Do not judge the future by the past. I did not
know of her existence. Now I do. It makes all the

difference in the world. I want to know my daughter and have her know me. Make no mistake about that!"

Was the fact he had a child just a novelty that he wanted to explore with the same enthusiasm he had attended football games at Berkeley or shared pizza at La Val's? A novelty to enjoy then walk away from without once looking back? Or would he want more? Would he ask for visitation? Was he planning to discuss custody? Would he actually go that far?

"Don't do this," she whispered, afraid of the determination she saw in his expression.

"*Chérie,* the time to not do something is long past, ten years long past. We do not need to be enemies. We were once lovers. Can we not at least be friends now?"

Or more than friends?

The attraction he'd felt for her from the first moment he'd met her remained strong. He hadn't lied when he'd told her he'd never forgotten her. He'd ached with wanting her for years.

He'd tried to assuage that longing with marriage to Sasela. Not even that had eased the craving he experienced for this woman.

He felt it still. Maybe he'd have to wait. Maybe he'd have the biggest battle of his life with his Chloe. But sooner or later, she would be his. As would his daughter. He wasn't sure what he would do if it never happened.

"Tomorrow, I'll see Mackenzie." Karif straightened and stepped back. Releasing his hold on Chloe, he reached for her wrist, clamped it in his hand and led her to the sofa. She sank onto it, looking lost, alone, and defeated.

Reaching for the phone, Karif never let his eyes drift

from her as he spoke. "Salid? Tell Fahim to have the limo out front in ten minutes."

Chloe shook her head, frantic for some way to prevent this. She didn't want him invading her life. She'd been reasonably content in recent years. He'd change everything.

And she feared for her daughter. What did he mean to do about her?

Karif hung up and sat down beside her, hemming her in. "Is my name on the birth certificate?"

She dropped her gaze to her hands, surprised to see how tightly she had clenched them. Taking a shaky breath, she licked her dry lips. "The father's listed as Ben Shakirah which is the name by which I knew you."

"That makes things easier."

"What things?"

"I don't have to prove that I'm her father."

Eight

The flowers greeted her when she arrived at her office at the *Sentinel* the next morning. They were still as fresh and vibrant as they'd been when delivered. Had it only been two days ago?

For a long moment, Chloe stared at them. So much had happened she felt as if a century had passed.

Studying them, she thought about what they could represent--being courted in an old-fashioned way. She wished the flowers had been bought with her happiness in mind. Instead, she felt besieged.

"No new flowers today," her friend Sheila said teasing, as she stopped in the opening to Chloe's cubicle.

One of the copy editors stopped by, grinning. "You should let us have those out here in the open, so everyone can enjoy them."

Chloe was tempted. Maybe she could think of something else besides Karif if the flowers weren't a constant reminder. But putting them out in the general area would give rise to even more comments.

Shaking her head, she forced a grin. "I'll keep them right here, thanks." She really wanted to toss them in the trash, but that would cause too much speculation.

"All right, get back to work. This is not some coffee klatch." Jack Mason strode through the newsroom and headed for Chloe's desk. The workers beside her parted for the editor-in-chief and Sheila drifted back to her desk.

"We were just admiring Chloe's flowers," Margot, a copy editor, said, standing her ground. "She got them the other day from a *friend*."

"Probably the same friend who took her to a reception last night," Mason said, slamming down a competitor's newspaper.

A picture of Chloe standing beside Karif in the receiving line filled a good third of the page.

"Oh." She stared at the picture unable to think of anything to say. The last thing she'd wanted was publicity or notoriety.

"You could've at least clued us in so we could have had a similar picture," Mason growled.

"Wow, Chloe, isn't he that oil sheikh that's been in the news recently?" Margot asked, her eyes avidly studying the photo.

"He's an old friend," Chloe mumbled, snatching the paper and folding it as if hiding the picture could hide the knowledge of it from the world.

Raising her head, Chloe forced herself to make eye contact with her co-workers. "I knew him years ago and when he found out I was in Washington, he invited me to this reception to visit a little. That's all."

She smiled and held her breath, praying that her explanation would satisfy them.

"Back to work." Waiting until Margot left, Mason faced Chloe. "Let me know next time you plan to attend a function with the newsworthy sheikh. We could use some of the pictures ourselves," he said, turning to head back to his office.

Mike stepped into Chloe's work area, a quick glance at Mason's back. Smiling slyly, he walked up to Chloe and tilted her chin up, assessing her with narrowed eyes.

"Is there a story here, Chloe?" he asked suspiciously.

She stepped away, irritated. "There's no story, Mike."

"Funny, you didn't mention knowing him the other day when we covered the speeches at the White House."

"I didn't know if he'd recognize me. It was ages ago when I knew him. I was surprised when he invited me to the reception." She shrugged, not wanting to go into all that had happened last night. She was desperately trying to forget it.

"You have to admit, I don't usually move in such exalted circles."

Mike studied her for a moment then nodded as if satisfied with her explanation. "Come on, then, mighty sidekick, I've got an assignment that cries out for good pictures," Mike said. But while his tone was jovial, his eyes remained watchful.

Glad to fall into the routine of work, Chloe flashed a relieved smile and followed Mike to their next assignment. She wanted to fill every minute with activity so she didn't have time to think about Karif.

It was later than normal when Chloe pulled into her driveway that evening. Fortunately, Mrs. Hanson wasn't a stickler about time. The elderly widow enjoyed

Mackenzie's company and never seemed to mind accommodating herself to Chloe's somewhat erratic schedule. She was like the grandmother Mackenzie would never know. Mrs. Hanson spent her holidays with them and they always remembered her on her birthday with a huge cake and a small gathering of neighbors.

"Hi, Chloe," Elsie Hanson greeted her when she opened the front door. "Long day?"

"Hi. Long and tiring. I think I'll turn in early and catch up on some sleep."

Last night's sleep had been fitful. Over and over again she'd replayed the scene where Karif confirmed he was Mackenzie's father. And the ominous words echoed, I *won't have to prove that I'm her father.*

"I didn't start dinner. You didn't let me know this morning," Mrs. Hanson said.

"I know. I didn't know what I wanted this morning, so I thought we'll order a pizza or something. Is Mackenzie home?" Chloe placed her bag on the table by the front door and glanced down the hall toward her daughter's room.

"No." Mrs. Hanson paused by the door. "She went for a ride with that distinguished man who was here the other evening. They should have been back by now. I didn't want to leave before you got home in case they returned."

She went to the table and picked up a folded note. Smiling brightly, she offered it to Chloe. "He left this. It was all right to let Mackenzie go with him, wasn't it?"

Trepidation splashed through Chloe. Unable to say a word, she nodded, the note almost burning her fingers.

"Goodbye, my dear, see you both tomorrow," Mrs. Hanson said.

Chloe watched the older woman leave, feeling slightly ill. Slowly she opened the note. *Don't worry, I have Mackenzie safe.* The scribble afterward had to be his name.

Don't worry? She was sick with worry. Her mind whirling, she gazed blindly around her living room. Where had he taken her daughter? Were they even now over the Atlantic on their way to the Arabian desert? Would she ever see her darling little girl again?

Chloe felt she was going to be sick. She tried her best to keep things low-key and he was doing his best to upset everything.

Walking to the sink in the kitchen, Chloe ran the water until it was cool, then filled a glass. Karif had no business taking Mackenzie without her permission. She swallowed the water, slamming the glass back on the counter, trying to calm her rioting nerves, quell the nausea that plagued her, slow her rapid pulse. She would not let him take her daughter!

In less than fifteen minutes, Chloe pulled up in front of the elegant old hotel where Karif and his entourage were staying. She left her car in the No Parking zone, ignoring the call of the doorman. Almost running, she hurried to the elevators.

Fear had changed to anger. When she got her hands on sheikh Karif bin Shakirah, she was going to strangle him! And make damn sure he knew to stay away from her daughter in the future.

When she spotted the men in the hall, she knew Karif and Mackenzie were here. Stepping into the hallway, she headed toward the room. Determined to get through, no matter what, she faced them brazenly.

"Sorry, ma'am, these rooms are private." One of the guards stepped out to bar the way.

"My name is Chloe McDonald and my daughter is there with the sheikh," she began, ready to battle anyone who dared stand in her way.

"Of course, madam. I am sorry I did not recognize you at first. This way. We were expecting you." The man bowed slightly, then led the way to the suite's door. Opening it, he stood aside.

Upon entering the luxurious suite, Chloe's eyes were instantly drawn to the tall man standing near the window.

Dressed in formal attire, his jacket slung across the back of a nearby chair, Karif looked at her when she burst in. The white shirt emphasized his rugged good looks. For a moment her breath caught at his masculine beauty. Before she could utter a word, however, Mackenzie sprang up from the sofa and hurried to her mother, a beaming smile on her face.

"Hi, Mom." She flung, her arms around Chloe.

Flicking an angry glance at Karif, Chloe knelt beside Mackenzie and returned her hug. "Hi, pumpkin. You okay?" she asked softly.

"Sure."

Karif remained by the window, silently watching them, his expression unreadable.

Chloe held her daughter, her eyes meeting Karif's. He stared back, wondering at the myriad expressions that chased across her face. Anger, certainly. He'd known she wouldn't like his taking Mackenzie for a visit. But was there also a trace of fear?

He frowned at that.

"Mom, today was awesome. I thought I was only going for a ride in the limo. Mrs. Hanson said I could. It was so cool. We rode around and I did just what you said waved to all the people on the sidewalk and pretended I was a princess."

Karif's lips twitched slightly. That's what that waving had been all about--he'd wondered.

Warily watching Chloe, he also wondered if he'd ever get the chance again to indulge Mackenzie in her fantasies. He stood a little straighter. He was Mackenzie's father and he would get to know his little girl.

"Then we came here, and I wasn't sure we should stay. I didn't want Mrs. Hanson to worry. But Karif said she knew I was with him and wouldn't worry. So we had ice cream from room service. I wish we could live in a hotel. They bring you whatever you want." Mackenzie's excitement and happiness shone on her face.

Chloe held on to her composure with iron will. She was furious with Karif. She'd been scared half out of her wits while he'd been indulging Mackenzie.

"Time to go home, now, pumpkin," Chloe said, facing Karif defiantly. Taking Mackenzie's hand firmly in hers she glanced once toward the door. Would anyone try to stop them if they left?

Karif crossed the room.

"How dare you!" Chloe said when he drew near.

He cocked an eyebrow in disbelief. "If you're referring to my inviting Mackenzie to spend the afternoon with me, you know perfectly well why I did so."

"You have no right to abduct her." Try as she might, the anger sounded in her voice. She wanted to rail at him for scaring her so, for daring to act as if spending the day with Mackenzie was the most natural thing in the world for him. It was not. It could not be. Chloe dare not let it.

"Abduct? Surely that's a bit strong." His voice sharpened as he stopped so close to Chloe she had to take a step back to meet his hard gaze.

"I have every right to spend time with her." His threat was implicit.

She shivered and took another step back. "She's my daughter and I say who she can see and when."

Mackenzie looked from her mother to Karif, puzzled.

"Perhaps you would care to be seated while we discuss this further?" Karif said politely, but the expression on his face was formidable.

"There's nothing further to discuss. We're leaving."

"Not just yet, you're not." He reached out and took her arm in a hard grasp. "It's past time to air the truth of this situation. You overreacted by storming in here."

"Overreacted?" She would show him overreacting. Yanking her arm free, she stepped forward, her eyes blazing mad. "You had no right to take my daughter, and if you ever do such a thing again without my knowledge and permission, I'll—"

"Do not speak to me about rights. I have as many as you and if you need me to prove that to you I'm willing to do so."

"Mom." Mackenzie tugged on Chloe's hand. "Mom, are we going?"

"In a minute."

Karif lifted Chloe's chin with a hard finger. "It's time to tell her, *cherie*. Either we do so together or I'll do it on my own. Which do you prefer?"

She hadn't wanted everything to blow up in her face, yet it looked as if it were about to.

This was not how or when she wanted to tell Mackenzie about her father.

Would he try to take Mackenzie away from her?

She needed time, time to decide how best to tell her.

"Aren't you on your way out?" Chloe asked, stalling for time, her heart tripping with fear. She didn't want to be in this situation. She'd had enough problems over the last ten years. She did not need this now.

"I'm expected at a small reception in a little while, but I certainly have time for this."

She pulled her chin away and looked around the room as if searching for an escape route. She'd been angry when she'd arrived. Now she was scared. She didn't want to talk with Karif. She just wanted to go home, close the door and shut out the world. Shut out the threat to her very existence.

"Not now."

"I want to spend time with her. When are you planning to tell her?"

"I certainly don't want to just blurt it out."

"There is no reason not to tell her the truth, Chloe. Past time, I'd say."

"I'll tell her."

"When?"

"Soon."

"No, Chloe, today. Now."

"Are you guys talking about me?" Mackenzie asked, trying to follow the conversation.

Karif's features softened as he smiled at Mackenzie. "Yes, sweetheart, we are. Your mother and I have something important to discuss with you." He glanced at his aide and made a motion with his head. In seconds the man left and only Chloe, Karif and Mackenzie remained in the room.

Chloe swallowed hard, her hand tightening involuntarily around Mackenzie's.

"Ow, Mom, you're squeezing me."

"Sorry, honey." It was an effort to relax her grip, an effort to breathe. Her heart was pounding loudly and she couldn't look away from Karif's compelling gaze.

She had to say no. She dare not let him appropriate Mackenzie whenever he felt like it. What kind of relationship would he build with Mackenzie? Here today and gone tomorrow? Would Mackenzie become so fascinated by the glamour of her father that she'd find her mother lacking? Would she grow dissatisfied with their life and wish to learn more about how her father lived?

She already was enchanted with limousines and room service. Would she be hurt when he left at the end of his visit?

Karif slowly raised Chloe's hand in his, holding it in a firm grip. Chloe felt the connection spread from her hand throughout her entire body. Her knees grew weak when he brought her fingertips to his lips and gently kissed each one.

"Now, *chérie*. Today," he repeated.

Her eyes were caught in his gaze, snared almost; she

wanted to look away yet was unable to.

"I'll have to think about it."

"There is nothing to think about. I can demand my rights, you know," he replied in a silky tone.

She yanked her fingers from his grasp. "No."

"I grow tired of your constantly telling me no."

It was time to end the charade. He wanted to know his daughter and he wanted her to know her father. He drew Chloe and Mackenzie to the sofa and waited while they sank down on the cushions. He took the chair across from them.

Chloe licked her lips. Slowly she turned to face her little girl.

"Mackenzie, honey," she said, reaching out to brush her hair back from her cheeks. "Remember when you were a little girl and I told you your daddy had gone away? That I didn't know what happened to him, but I thought maybe he died?"

Mackenzie nodded, her eyes firmly on her mother's face.

"Well, I didn't know for sure. I thought so because he went away and never contacted me. But he didn't die."

Mackenzie looked to Karif and then back to Chloe.

"In fact, he came here to Washington and found us and--"

"It's Karif, isn't it?" Mackenzie guessed.

"Yes, honey, Karif is your father. He didn't know where we were living. He didn't know you were born."

"If I had, I would have come to see you immediately. I'm thankful now that I found you and your mother," Karif said.

Nine

"So do I have to go live with him now?" Mackenzie asked.

"Of course not, you're still my little girl. You live with me," Chloe replied quickly.

"You don't know me very well, Mackenzie, but I want us to spend more time together so we can get to know each other. I had a nice time this afternoon with you. I'd like to spend more time with you while I'm here."

"I don't know," Chloe warned.

"I will spend time with my daughter, Chloe. Nothing you do or say can stop me. You can only alter how it happens. Because of the trade treaty and my country's huge reserves of oil, your government doesn't want to harm the relationship between our countries. Don't tempt me to use that power to exercise my rights."

One phone call would do it, Chloe knew. She rose impatiently and paced to the window. She hated this. She thought she had her life in control, now it was spinning out of control and she was helpless to do anything about it.

Karif spoke softly to Mackenzie then crossed to stand close to Chloe. He reached out to caress her shoulders, as if trying to ease some of the tension. Chloe felt the warmth of his breath move lightly over her cheek as he drew her closer to him.

"I—" She couldn't think.

"You what?" he coaxed.

"I thought you'd taken her back to your country," she said in a rush.

He frowned and spun her around. "Kidnaped her, you mean?" Gone was the gentle tone in his voice.

Chloe shivered and nodded.

"That's a great thought. You really think I'm capable of such a despicable act? When I want something, I tell people exactly what I want. I have no need to kidnap my own daughter. I can easily petition your courts to gain visitation rights, maybe even full custody."

She paled at his words. "Last night, you made such a big thing out of wanting to get to know Mackenzie, that when I came home today and found her gone I thought—"

"You thought I had taken a child from the only home she knows? And to go off with a man she just met? If I had known about her before last night, I'd have tried to get to know her earlier. Why am I the villain in this because I wish to get to know my own daughter?"

"You're not a villain. It's just hard to believe you want to get to know a child. You do have a certain international reputation—" She closed her eyes, tried again, "I'm not used to sharing her. I was afraid you would take her away. Face it, Karif, you have more money than I'll ever see. You're influential, powerful, ruthless—"

"Ruthless enough to take a child from her mother

without either's consent? Were you ever going to tell me about her? If I hadn't guessed, would you ever have told me?"

He released her and stepped back. Thrusting both his hands into his pockets, he turned to stare out of the window, anger evident in every inch of his stance.

"You said it yourself earlier, I don't know you, Karif. In truth, I never did. The man I thought I knew doesn't exist. I can only judge things by what I know. Ten years ago you disappeared without a word," she tried to explain.

"I told you what happened. If I want my daughter, I have no need to kidnap her."

Chloe nodded at the truth of that statement. Fear lapped at her senses. Was he planning to petition the courts? With the full force of the United States government behind him, he'd have no trouble getting whatever he wanted.

She watched him warily, afraid as she'd never been before.

He glanced at her and felt the familiar tightening deep in his gut at the sight of her. She was so beautiful. He wanted her with a hunger more suitable to some randy teenager than a man in his mid-thirties.

And he obviously wanted her more than she wanted him. Even the fact that she had concealed their daughter from him no longer mattered.

As he studied hers, he realized she was afraid.

"There's a certain truth in what you said earlier," he conceded.

"Huh?" Chloe was so confused and afraid, she didn't know what he was talking about.

"You don't know me now. Nor do I know you. So I propose we change that."

"Change it how?" she asked warily.

"We'll get to know each other again, of course. What did you think I meant?"

"I don't know. How will we get to know each other?"

"By seeing each other while I'm in Washington."

"To what end?"

He made an impatient gesture. "I don't know. Does it have to be toward some end? Can't I just learn about you and Mackenzie, see what you've done with your lives and give you the same opportunity to learn about mine? I'll spend time with Mackenzie. I'm asking you to join us. You can refuse if you wish."

"No, I'll go along," she said quickly before he could change his mind.

"Afraid to leave Mackenzie alone with me?" He taunted.

Meeting his gaze squarely, she nodded.

Looking into his eyes made her body tingle. Forgotten yearnings blossomed. She wished she wasn't afraid to take what he offered--a limited friendship for the time he was in Washington.

She didn't have time for wild fantasies about a romantic interlude.

She was surprised he wanted to spend any time with her. It was Mackenzie he was interested in seeing. And she couldn't let herself forget it.

"We had something special once," Karif reminded her.

"It was magic and the magic's gone," she replied,

refusing to be swept away by memories. "I have to get home. I'm tired, Mackenzie's tired. It's getting late. We still have dinner to get."

"Did you drive here or shall I have Fahim take you home?"

"I drove." Suddenly she remembered she'd just left her car where she had stopped it. She hoped it was still there.

"I'll come tomorrow night to take you both to dinner. Be ready at six."

Chloe didn't want this. She wanted things to go back to how they'd been last week. Was it only a few days since her entire world had been turned upside down?

She was trying to hold on to sanity, but Karif wasn't making things easy. She was trying to protect her little girl. Karif would be leaving soon.

Mackenzie could be badly hurt. She herself could be hurt. Chloe would do anything to protect her baby. For herself it was already a decade too late.

"Mackenzie's not used to eating in restaurants that have slow service. It would be better to eat at home," she said, reluctantly agreeing to his demands.

"All the better. We can talk and I can see where she lives, where you live."

"You've been to the house."

"But not been shown through it. And I'll tell you about my house and how my rooms compare to yours," he said.

"All right, at six, then." Turning, Chloe crossed the room to her daughter. "Ready, pumpkin? Time to go."

Mackenzie peeked at Karif. "Bye."

"Bye, Mackenzie. I will see you tomorrow."

By six o'clock the next next evening, Chloe's nerves were frazzled. She debated all afternoon what to prepare for dinner, knowing she was not the world's best cook. Also knowing Karif probably had dozens of chefs who prepared his meals.

Instead, she tried a different tactic. She ordered a large pizza, tossed a salad and made a sinfully rich dessert they could have with coffee.

She felt as nervous as a schoolgirl on her first date which wasn't all due to his determination to get to know Mackenzie.

Some was her own anticipation at seeing him again.

She couldn't forget the circumstances of their separation. Despite that, she was totally intrigued by the man. He wore his cloak of authority and power comfortably. She'd seen traces of it in Berkeley, but never knew what it would lead to.

She did want to know more about him. To learn what he'd done in the intervening years. Could she find out without risking her heart?

Chloe was wiping the counters in the kitchen, cleaning up from the preparation of the salad, when Mackenzie wandered in.

"He's here," she said, pausing at the doorway.

"He?" Chloe asked.

"The limo's out front."

Chloe glanced at her daughter. They had spoken very little last night on the ride home and Mackenzie had gone straight to bed once she'd finished dinner.

After school today, she went home with Stephie. She'd only been back a few minutes.

Neither of them had broached the subject of Karif. What was her daughter thinking now? How did she feel having discovered that Karif was her father?

Should she have told Mackenzie once Karif contacted her?

She had so hoped to keep it secret.

"Sweetie, later you and I will talk about Karif, okay?" she asked her daughter.

Watching her mother from solemn eyes, Mackenzie nodded.

The house seemed to shrink when Karif's presence filled it. He seemed larger than life, Chloe thought, as she gazed around her living room and tried to remember it without him in it.

He'd dressed casually in brown slacks and a dark blue shirt. Fleetingly, she wondered if he ever wore jeans as he had in college.

"I didn't cook tonight. I ordered a pizza. Have you had any since you've left?" Chloe asked when he stepped into the livingroom.

"Pizza sounds good. I haven't had any in a long time. Do you like pizza, Mackenzie?"

She nodded, staying near her mother, her eyes watching Karif with fascination.

"I'll set the dining room table. The pizza should be here any minute," Chloe said, anxious to have something to do to avoid the stilted conversation.

"Do you normally eat in the dining room or are you

doing so solely for my benefit?" he asked.

She met his eyes. "For special occasions."

"I'd rather eat where you normally eat."

They ate pizza and salad at the kitchen table.

As the meal progressed, Chloe gradually began to relax.

"Not as good as La Val's or is memory playing tricks on me?" Karif asked as he tasted his first piece. La Val's had been their favorite pizza place when they lived in Berkeley.

"No. I haven't found any other pizza as good as La Val's," Chloe agreed. "I don't know, maybe it's just the memories. Maybe it wasn't all that good."

"We should go back some day and try it."

Her gaze dropped to her own piece. *We should go back some day,* as if they'd be together in the future.

Don't count on fairy tales, she reminded herself. And don't forget Karif was a man she didn't really know.

"What's La Val's?" Mackenzie asked.

"A great pizza place in Berkeley that your mother and I often frequented," Karif answered easily. Not for him any of the awkwardness that surrounded the meal.

"*Frequented* is the right word. As I remember, some weeks we ate there three nights," Chloe said with a smile.

"I never had such good pizza before. In fact, I don't believe I had eaten pizza before," he explained.

"Don't you have pizza where you live?" Mackenzie asked, obviously unable to imagine a place that didn't have a staple such as pizza.

He nodded. "We do now. But ten years ago we didn't. Coming to America was a very educational experience for me."

"Let's see, there was pizza and beer, football and—" Chloe broke off, remembering how enthralled Karif had been in so many things she'd taken for granted.

"Pom-pom girls," he supplied, wicked amusement gleaming.

"Is that why you liked football so much?" she asked in mock outrage.

He smiled, his eyes warm and penetrating. "No, but it was a good part of the experience."

"And what about the beer? I thought sheikhs didn't drink."

"Only strict Muslims. You forget, my mother's French. Do you think I could get away without learning all there is about wine? But beer--"

He shook his head, smiling down at Mackenzie. "Never drink beer with college kids. I was sick for two days afterward the first time I tried to keep up."

Mackenzie giggled, her gaze darting back and forth between her mother and father, clearly entranced with the exchange, the glimpse of their lives before she was born.

She was growing more relaxed around Karif Chloe could see.

"So tell us about all the other educational experiences you've had," Chloe urged, longing to keep the conversation light. She didn't want to talk about what she dreaded most, Karif and Mackenzie.

"Let's see." Karif addressed Mackenzie, "You must understand, most of my previous schooling had been in Europe. I wasn't used to brash American slang, hot dogs, professors who wore blue jeans to class, a fountain named for a dog and the sassy free spirit of American girls. I enjoyed it. So don't ever let anyone tell you education can be boring. I was never bored."

His eyes caught Chloe's on the last, held.

Chloe finished her pizza. She reached for the large soda bottle at the same time Karif did. His fingers covered hers. For a long moment they sat motionless, each looking at the other. Slowly he drew his hand away.

"I'll pour yours." Was that breathless voice hers?

Hoping her hand wouldn't tremble, she filled his glass, then her own. Setting the bottle down with a thunk, she was annoyed at herself for reacting so strongly merely to the touch of his fingertips.

Flustered, Chloe didn't realize she was staring at him until he asked if he had spilled something.

"No. I was just thinking that eating in the kitchen is not something you probably do much of," she blurted out, hoping to divert any suspicions that her thoughts were on a different track.

Karif smiled. "Not at home. But sometimes I spend time in the desert, especially now that we've found the oil reserve. Then I stay in a Bedouin tent. Even with carpets on the sand, grit infiltrates everything. At least there's no sand here."

"You stay in a tent? Do you ride camels?" Mackenzie asked.

"Horses--purebred Arabians. Some of the Bedouins have camels, but I've never liked riding them."

"But you have?" she persisted, her eyes wide.

"Yes. But I prefer horses. Do you ride?"

Mackenzie shook her head.

"Time you learned," Karif said.

"Riding lessons cost money," Chloe said without thinking. She didn't want Karif suggesting things she would have to follow through on. Money and time were tight. She had all she could do to allow Mackenzie to play in the school soccer league. She couldn't manage riding lessons. Facing him, she strengthened her resolve even though she felt as if things were sliding out of her control.

Ten

Karif wasn't used to being frustrated. With Chloe, it was becoming a way of life. For every step forward, he took two back.

Chloe had begun to relax. He knew the reminiscences of Berkeley had been responsible. Things between them had begun to improve, now she had re-erected her walls ten feet tall.

How was he to get close to her if she wouldn't let him? He smiled grimly. He'd thought finding her would be the difficult part. That had been amazingly simple-- she'd just appeared. The hard part was convincing her to trust him enough to let him back into her life.

"I can pay for Mackenzie to learn to ride," he said easily.

Chloe paused in reaching for her glass, her eyes met his. "No, thank you."

"I'd like to learn to ride a horse," Mackenzie said shyly.

"And so you shall." Karif held Chloe's gaze, his own strong and sure.

"That's not for you to decide," Chloe said tightly.

Karif cocked an eyebrow. "Are you suggesting that

just because I don't live in Washington, I can have no place in Mackenzie's future?" he asked in a deceptively calm voice.

Chloe looked at her daughter's avid gaze. "If you're finished, Mackenzie, you may go outside and ride your bike."

"I want to stay here and watch you two fight," Mackenzie said.

"We're not fighting," Chloe said calmly, though the anger that roiled inside her gave the lie to her words. She wanted to scream at Karif to leave them alone, to go back to his desert kingdom and let her and her daughter resume their lives as they'd been before his arrival last week.

Mackenzie looked doubtful.

"Your mother's correct, we're having a discussion, that's all. Adults can have strong discussions without fighting," Karif said.

Chloe fumed silently. If he'd leave, there'd be no fight. But if he thought she'd quietly acquiesce to all his demands, he was in for the fight of his life!

Mackenzie looked back and forth at her parents. "I guess I'll go see if Stephie can ride now."

"Stay out front where we can check on you," Chloe said.

The silence grew in the kitchen when she left. Karif leaned back in his chair, tipping it on its back legs, watching Chloe with brooding eyes.

She stared at the table, unsure how to begin. She had to make her point clearly and succinctly. Yet she hesitated.

"Come on." He pushed away suddenly and stood up reaching for her hand.

"Where are we going?" Startled, she rose, her fingers tightening with his.

"Into the living room. It'll be more comfortable. I want to tell you about my father."

When they were seated on the sofa, Chloe tugged on her hand, Karif tightened his grip and rested their linked hands on his thigh. He looked at her through lowered lashes.

"My father married my mother despite opposition from his own father. If you remember your history, you'll remember that the French ruled my country for years. We were gaining our autonomy at the time my father and mother met, so you can imagine the strong anti-French feelings that abounded. Despite everything, all the objections of both families, my father married her. Theirs was not an easy nor happy marriage."

"Did your grandfather ever come around?" she asked, intrigued by what he was saying, though a bit puzzled as to why he was telling her all this.

"A bit, after I was born. And more and more so after each son. But my parents' marriage was never easy. When my father learned I was in love with an American, he did his best to persuade me that further involvement would be a mistake. While he'd loved my mother when they married, he lived with all the difficulties of such a marriage and he didn't want the same problems for me."

"So he intercepted your letters," Chloe said. It explained why, even deathly ill, the old man had found the strength to interfere.

"That and more. As my father's health improved, I became more and more worried about you. I tried to call, but your number had been disconnected. I wrote, sent telegrams, all to no avail. Finally, I hired an investigation firm to locate you."

"When?"

"It was late summer by then. I wish I could explain how hectic things were at that point, with my father's illness and the turmoil it brought. By then, I was frantic for news of you. You thought I'd disappeared without a trace, I felt the same about you. By that time, I'd had no word of you or from you for almost three months."

"I guess I moved by the time you hired the investigators."

"They found your father," Karif said slowly.

She blinked. "He didn't know where I'd gone."

He hadn't wanted to know where she was going or how she was going to manage. He'd washed his hands of her. The old pain was only a dull ache now. She accepted that aspect of the situation years ago.

"I know. Nor did he tell my investigator that you were pregnant. If I'd known, I would have moved heaven and earth to find you."

"What did he say?"

"What he said and what I was told he said were two different things. My father intercepted the report by the investigation firm. I found the original report after my father died last year. What I was given ten years ago was a report stating that your father said you didn't want to be bothered."

"Oh, Karif." Chloe's fingers tightened with his as she thought of how strongly his father had opposed their relationship. So strongly opposed he'd lied and manipulated things to get his own way. Would it have made a difference if the old man had known she was carrying Karif's child?

That was something she'd never know.

Now it was too late. Too much had happened over the intervening years for her to recapture the trust and love of years ago.

And it was obvious Karif didn't feel the same toward her. He'd married, tried to start a family. She sighed softly for the lost love she'd once thought held such a bright future.

"Thank you for telling me, it explains a lot," Chloe said softly.

"Now that you know this, what more do you need to know?" he asked.

"For?"

"To give us a chance, see if we can pick up where we left off. I can take care of you and Mackenzie better than you're doing. Come back home with me!"

She tugged her hand harder, the brief feeling of nostalgia fleeing as he so arrogantly stated his wishes. What of hers?

"Did I say I enjoyed sassy free-spirited American women? I lied. I want you agreeable to whatever I suggest," he said.

She glared at him. "I'm sure you do. Think a minute, Karif. You're a gazillionaire and can get away with anything you want. I, on the other hand, am a career woman, a single mother to boot. I have to watch our finances, be careful to provide for the future. I have a daughter to protect."

And a once-shattered heart to shelter.

"If I offer marriage, would that suit you?" His eyes narrowed as he watched her.

Her heart pounded in glorious happiness. *Marriage.* Just as they'd talked about so long ago.

Then reality crashed down. He'd said nothing of love or commitment or even simple caring. He wanted his daughter. On his terms. Was this a way to get his way?

"No, thank you," she said.

"Why not? Don't you trust that I—" He stopped. He nodded. "You don't trust me, do you, *chérie?*"

She shook her head. "No. I don't trust you, nor do I trust my own instincts about us. I loved you so much. You'll never know how hard I took your disappearance. You've reappeared, but for how long? And how would your family greet your marriage to me? We both know your father didn't want it. How would the rest of your family feel today?"

Nothing he'd said convinced her.

"What if there's another crisis? What if you have to suddenly leave again? Will I be left behind again without a word for another ten years? Have you told me the truth this time? All the truth? Or will I find out again that you lied? I'm not willing to take the risk."

"Chloe, think. I know where you live now and you won't be going anywhere. You know where I am, you could contact me if anything unexpected like that ever happened again. My father's dead. I run our country now, small as it is. There's no one to interfere. I kept my identity secret to fit in at Berkeley. You know my identity now. There were no other lies. That was a safety issue for me at the time."

She'd thought they were so close, couldn't he have trusted her?

"Circumstances are not the same, never will be again. I understand your hesitancy. But do you understand my determination?"

"You want your daughter."

"Yes."

"You can visit her whenever—"

"Not enough, Chloe. I've missed the first nine years of her life. Time passes too swiftly to be satisfied with a day's visit here and there when I am able to come to the United States. I want to spend the next nine years with her."

"You can't just take her away from me." Her deepest fear was spoken.

"I don't need to do that. I want you to come, too. If you need time to reach that same conclusion, I'm willing to give it to you."

"I don't--"

He shifted on the sofa, released her hand and drew her into his lap, his strong arms encircling her, holding her against his chest.

"Yes, Chloe, I want my daughter and her mother." His mouth lowered to hers.

Chloe wanted to resist. She longed to be able to show him how little he meant to her.

But her body betrayed her, responding instantly to the delight of his touch. Her lips opened to his and her tongue met his. Shimmering waves of pleasure lapped at her senses. Her arms crept up around his neck and she threaded her fingers in his thick dark hair, reveling in the sexy feel of him as his kiss deepened.

For a moment, she was nineteen again and so much in love.

Despite being afraid of letting her emotions rule, she felt momentarily wild and free and almost safe. She should be stronger than this, should stop his attempts to seduce her into compliance. Yet she felt helpless to resist. She'd yearned for his touch so many times over the years.

His kisses seduced her into traitorous thoughts. Dare she risk enjoying their time together knowing she would have to let go when he left? Dare she risk her heart again knowing how it would all end--if not when he left Washington this time then when Mackenzie was grown?

Had she ever stopped loving this man?

He eased her back, his eyes glittering with suppressed emotion. Gently, his index finger traced her damp lips.

Chloe flushed with embarrassment at having responded so freely. She tried to pull away, but his arms wouldn't let her go.

She should have been stronger--should have resisted!

"I must leave now. I'll pick you up for the symphony on Friday around seven."

She shook her head.

"Please agree that we'll spend some time getting to know each other again--for Mackenzie's sake, if nothing else."

Maybe she could find a way through this morass by then. She nodded. "All right, for Mackenzie's sake."

"I have one more function to attend this weekend, then my official visit will be over."

She held her breath. The piercing pain that shot through her was totally unexpected. She'd known all along he wouldn't be here long.

"After that I'll be on my own," he added.

And what exactly did that mean?

"So I'll see you Friday," she said brightly, pushing away, striving to hide the turmoil that filled her. The end of the week he'd be finished. There was nothing to keep him here beyond that except Mackenzie.

What could she do to keep her daughter safe, not risk her going off to some country she'd hardly heard of?

Chloe watched him walk to the limo from her front porch, wanting a promise that things would be different than the last time, but knowing there were no guarantees in life.

For a moment, she was almost willing to let go and grab all the happiness he offered for however brief a time. But she knew the price of such happiness and she didn't think she could pay it a second time.

Mackenzie rode up on her bike and stopped near the limo. "Are you coming to see me again?" she asked.

"I'll see you Friday night when I come to pick up your mother. We're going to the symphony." Karif paused by his daughter, taking in her shining eyes, her pretty brown curls. She looked so much like her mother his heart caught.

Mackenzie wrinkled her nose. "That's that slow music that Mom's always listening to on the radio."

Karif chuckled and nodded. "Yes, we both enjoy it. You might like it yourself one day. On Saturday, we'll do something together. You decide where you'd like to go or what you want to do."

"Okay." She waved shyly and turned to ride down the sidewalk to rejoin Stephanie.

"Don't hurt her," Chloe said involuntarily. She wasn't the only one involved now. Chloe couldn't bear to have her baby hurt.

Karif turned toward the house. "It has never been my intention to hurt either one of you," he stated.

Eleven

Karif slammed the car door, motioning Fahim to drive. He normally didn't display his temper in that manner. But his frustration was growing. He knew he had a hard fight ahead of him. Chloe was proving much more stubborn than he'd remembered. He wasn't averse to a relationship with a strong woman, but he wanted her strength on his side not opposed to him.

Now the only thing that mattered was convincing Chloe that she and their daughter could make a family with him.

With a twist of pain he realized how much he'd missed of Mackenzie's life. He'd missed seeing Chloe pregnant with their child. Missed seeing her nursing their baby. Missed Mackenzie's first steps, first day of school.

Never suspecting he'd left a child behind, he regretted so much. He wanted to have other children, ones he'd see from birth to adulthood. Would it help make up for missing all that with MacKenzie?

He had to hold on to the thought that they would have more. He wanted to convince Chloe to give them a second chance--and get to know his daughter in the process.

Time would do it. But it was in short supply.

He had a couple more weeks he could spare to stay in the United States, but then he had to return home and begin work on the new agreement.

He hoped he wasn't going to return home alone.

Before he left, he had to convince Chloe to join him.

"That dress is pretty, Mom," Mackenzie said when Chloe stepped into the living room Friday night.

The dress she'd chosen for tonight was a deep rose. The soft drape of the bodice plunged into a vee in front, modestly covering her figure, yet hinting at what lay beneath. The skirt flowed around her hips, brushing against her legs as she walked. The dress made her feel sexy just moving in it.

It also gave her a certain confidence she desperately needed.

Nervously, Chloe went to answer the doorbell when it rang. Mrs. Hanson stood on the stoop, smiling cheerfully.

"My, don't you look nice, Chloe. That dress's beautiful. Wherever did you get it?"

"Come in, Elsie. Margie Anderson helped me pick it out. We went to the mall last night. I appreciate your watching Mackenzie tonight."

"I'm glad to do it. We were getting into that jigsaw puzzle this afternoon. This gives us a chance to finish it."

When the doorbell rang again, Chloe knew it was Karif.

Mackenzie ran to the door, then greeted him shyly,

still obviously uncertain about his place in her life.

"Mackenzie, I brought you a present," Karif said.

"A present? What?" Mackenzie moved closer, clearly intrigued.

He merely smiled at her and held out a small box. She took it and opened it. Nestled inside on white cotton was a gold locket, with a small diamond in the center.

Lifting the delicate chain, Mackenzie stared at it, her eyes wide with wonder.

"It's so pretty."

"It's the kind that holds pictures," he said.

"Oh, Karif, it's lovely." Chloe would never spoil her daughter's pleasure, but she worried he'd spent too much on a piece of jewelry her young daughter might not be ready for.

"And for you, Chloe." He held out a long narrow box.

Chloe stared at it for a long moment. "I don't need a present," she said, staring at it warily.

He reached for her hand turned it palm up and placed the box in it.

"From me to you."

Chloe swallowed and opened the lid. The shimmering light that struck her from the delicate bracelet was like living fire. Every spectrum of the rainbow reflected. It was beautiful. She loved it.

"Wow, Mom, those look like diamonds!" Mackenzie said, peering into the box.

"Oh, Karif, I can't take diamonds," Chloe said, stricken.

He went still. "Why not?"

"I—it's too much. I can't accept." She offered the

box back. He made no move to touch it.

"You accepted the flowers I sent to your work." His tone was cool.

"That's different." Her fingers began to tremble. She didn't want to drop the box--why wouldn't he take it?

"How?"

"Well, for one thing, they didn't cost a small fortune." She felt defensive.

He hesitated a moment, his expression softening, then he smiled. Her eyes focused first on his dimple, then rose to meet his warm gaze.

Reaching out to brush a strand of hair back from her cheek, his said softly. "Indulge me, *chérie*. I wanted to buy you something that would remind you of me. I noticed you wore no jewelry the other night. Take the bracelet. It will go with anything. I didn't spend a lot on it. It's really a token."

Chloe looked at the box, then opened it again and studied the bracelet once more. Carefully, she took it out and wrapped it around her wrist. She let him fasten it. It was beautiful. The delicate gold work was a piece of art, the diamonds sparkled and shimmered as they caught the light.

"Thank you, I shall always cherish it," she said softly.

Tears pricked behind her lids. Was this a bribe--or a farewell gift?

"Thank you for my locket. I can't wait to show Stephie," Mackenzie said, turning toward the door.

"Not tonight, but you can call her if you like," Chloe said, hoping to come back down to earth. Her skin still tingled from Karif's fingers.

"Ah, Mom, I wouldn't be gone for long and it's still light outside," Mackenzie protested, moving toward the door, a cautious eye on her mother.

"*Pardonnez-moi, mon petit chou,* but I do not find it appropriate that you argue with your mother when she has forbidden you something," Karif said sternly.

Mackenzie looked at him for a long moment, then at her mother. She moved toward Mrs. Hanson.

"Sorry, Mom. I'll call her. Can she come over here if her mother lets her?"

"That's up to Mrs. Hanson. We're leaving now, give me a kiss goodbye."

Chloe was surprised she didn't resent that Karif had stepped in. He was the child's father, granted, but Chloe was used to dealing with Mackenzie herself. Yet she suspected he wouldn't spoil Mackenzie as she'd thought he might, to make up for the years apart.

It was oddly unsettling.

Salid stood by the limousine when Karif and Chloe emerged from the house. He opened the door and calmly greeted Chloe.

"Salid attends with us tonight," Karif explained when the door closed behind him. Salid sat in the front seat with Fahim. Both men wore the short *kalfiyeh,* the loose head scarf held in place by decorative cords.

"As a bodyguard?" Chloe guessed.

Karif shrugged. "It is customary for me to have him with me. He'll enjoy the music as well. What pictures did you take today?"

They discussed her work on the short drive to the Kennedy Center for the Performing Arts. Chloe tried to relax, tried to tell herself it was just a date between old friends. But she felt as if she were sitting on the edge of a precipice the entire time.

The Kennedy Center was crowded when they arrived. Fahim easily maneuvered through the traffic, dropping them off close to the main doors.

The crowd inside was already moving to take their seats when Chloe, Karif and Salid entered. Chloe spotted a Southern senator just as he saw Karif. In only moments they were discussing the different aspects of the recently signed treaty. The senator's young wife shook her head at Chloe.

"Always shoptalk. Don't you get tired of it?"

Chloe smiled and gave a noncommittal shrug. She was fascinated by it and much too new at this to be at all upset by it.

She also knew she was living a fairy tale. When Karif's business was finished in Washington, he'd return home and she'd return to her job as a newspaper photographer.

But for the moment, she decided to enjoy the fantasy for all it was worth.

"Sorry about that," Karif said softly as he took her arm to lead her to their seats. Nodding to two other acquaintances, he waited while Salid produced the tickets to the ushers at the door.

"Part of your job, I assume," Chloe said.

"I certainly would do nothing to upset one of your senators, if that's what you mean."

"I think I meant always being available to people. Having to stop and talk even when you're taking an evening for yourself."

"I don't do much of this, so it's not a burden. Ah, are we ready Salid?"

"Yes, Excellency, this way, I believe."

As they made their way down the hall toward the seats, Chloe thought about all the burdens Karif carried on his broad shoulders. It was hard to remember he was no longer the carefree college student she'd known. He had a tremendous amount of responsibility now.

Did he consider her just another burden in his list of responsibilities?

Chloe sat in the opulent setting and looked around her with thinly veiled excitement. It'd been years since she'd attended the symphony. She loved music of all kinds but especially the classics.

She was amazed at the number of people she recognized. Some were from pictures she'd shot for the paper, some from other pictures in the paper. Washington's elite were gathered tonight and she was part of it.

She smiled at Karif, happy in his company, in the night, happy with everything at the moment.

Salid settled behind Karif, between the sheikh and the door. His eyes never settled on anything, but were constantly moving searching out any possible danger. Chloe glanced at him for a moment, then looked thoughtfully at Karif, her smile fading.

"Is your life threatened in any way?" she asked softly.

Karif leaned forward slightly until his shoulder brushed against hers. His dark eyes looked deep into hers. "The only danger is what I experience around you," he said seductively.

She flushed with heat. Her heart rate doubled. "I meant, because Salid is always with you."

Karif nodded. "It's more tradition than necessity. My life has never been threatened. But members of the *sajine* always accompany the sheikh. The tradition goes back generations. Does his presence bother you?"

She shook her head unable to look away from the heat of his dark eyes. She was relieved by his answer. She didn't want him to be in danger. Didn't want anything to threaten his well-being.

Her heart didn't stop pounding. She wanted only the best for him, always had, despite all that had gone before them.

"If it does, I'll send him away," Karif said, his hand covering hers as it rested in her lap. Lacing his fingers through hers, he drew their linked hands to his thigh. Slowly his thumb traced patterns against her wrist.

"Don't," Chloe whispered. The desire that sprang up at his touch was instant and insistent. She wanted to be closer, wanted to feel his lips against hers again, wanted more than he could ever again offer her.

"Chérie, there is more that I want, but this very public place is not conducive to that. I will resign myself to holding your hand. Until later."

"Later?" Chloe could scarcely form a coherent thought. His touch was driving her crazy.

"I planned a midnight supper at my hotel. It'll afford us the privacy a restaurant would not."

"I need to get home after this. I don't want to go to your hotel."

"Shh, we can discuss it after the symphony. They are

preparing to begin," he said as the house lights slowly dimmed.

Between the diamond bracelet on her left wrist and Karif's hand holding her right one, Chloe felt surrounded by him. His presence invaded her senses. Around him she felt desired, cherished. He could be charming, there was no denying that.

He could also be ruthless. She'd seen glimpses of it, and hadn't he admitted he would do whatever he had to in order to get his own way?

The music was beautiful. The acoustics perfect for the delightful enjoyment of the orchestra's rendition of the familiar pieces. Chloe began to relax and enjoy the treat.

Conscious every second of Karif beside her, she was still able to forget the turmoil that plagued her and give herself up to the beauty of the romantic composers the orchestra played.

At intermission they wandered out to the grand foyer of the Kennedy Center. Several well-known men stopped to greet Karif.

Senators, White House staff, a general expanded their circle. Karif conversed easily with everyone. He was never at a loss for words, always charming and seemed to have the ability to remember everyone's name and position. Chloe saw the curious glances at their linked hands, but no one questioned it.

She spoke to each as they were introduced, but left the conversation to Karif. These men were here to woo the visiting sheikh who was so generous with his oil, not to talk to her.

She didn't mind. She was fascinated by this side of the

man.

Scanning the area, she was pleased to note there were no photographers present. She did not need to fuel the gossip that the last picture had started.

Listening with only half an ear to the conversations that swirled around, Chloe tried to imagine being a part of this all the time as Karif was.

She was enjoying herself, but only because of Karif.

"Not too bad, was it?" he asked her when they returned to their seats.

She smiled and shook her head. "It was fun. I've never met so many congressmen."

"I'm sure each one envied me because you were with me."

"I'm sure they were wondering who I was but were just too polite to ask," she returned dryly, charmed with his compliment in spite of herself.

He raised their linked hands and kissed the back of each of her fingers. "Come to the hotel for a late supper," he coaxed.

She hesitated, then nodded. She didn't want the evening to end when the music stopped. She wanted the evening to go on a little longer.

He was right, it would be more private in his suite than in a crowded restaurant. At least they'd not have a constant stream of people interrupting.

Though Chloe feared she was flirting with danger to spend time alone with Karif, especially in such a romantic setting as the elegant sitting room of his suite at the Williams. She'd agreed to go for supper--that was all.

Karif smiled with satisfaction and settled back to

enjoy the rest of the evening. He was pleased with the way the night was going.

Chloe had fit in perfectly at his side. She'd held her own with the men he'd spoken with, hadn't been shy or uncertain as Sasela so often had been.

Chloe was a strong, confident woman. He liked that about her. Among other things, he thought as he slanted a glance in her direction.

She was gazing rapturously at the orchestra, her eyes sparkling in the dim light, a delighted smile curving her lips.

Karif wanted to capture those lips with his, draw a response as she had the last time he kissed her.

The years had treated her kindly, her complexion was fresh and young, untouched by time. Highlights in her hair caught the faint light and shone beneath it. He wanted to thread his fingers through those curls and relish their soft silky texture.

He regretted the loss of the long silky hair he'd so loved, but it was still beautiful. He wanted to feel it against his skin again, brush it and tangle his fingers in the silky waves.

Shifting slightly, he looked at the orchestra. He needed to keep his thoughts on the music and not on the woman beside him. He had time later that night to get her to change her mind. To give them a chance—him a chance.

When they were in the limo, heading for the Williams Hotel, doubts began to plague her. She should have insisted on returning home. She didn't need any more time with him. It was starting to confuse her.

"Tell me about Manasia," she blurted out. If she could keep him talking, maybe some of the doubts would fade.

"What do you wish to know?" he asked.

"What's it like? I've never been to that area of the world. Is it all desert? Or do you have oases?"

He chuckled softly. "It's a beautiful country. Long and narrow, we have a variety of topography, from the sparkling white shores of the Mediterranean to the harsh dunes of the Sahara. There're a few oases scattered in the desert, made all the more beautiful for being surrounded by endless miles of golden sand."

"You said you live near the Mediterranean."

"My villa has an expanse of shore, soft white sand and a gentle slope that goes out many yards into the water before shelving down enough for swimming. It's perfect for children. My nephews safely play in the shallows. Older children and adults can swim there, as well."

"It sounds nice."

Like heaven, she thought. As a child, she'd spent many hours at Balboa Beach in southern California. She missed it. Washington was too far inland to visit the beach often.

"My villa's large, with lots of glass to give the feeling of being outdoors. I like to be outside and when it's not possible, I still want to feel like I am."

"Do you have a garden? What grows there?" she asked, trying to envision his home. He'd seen hers, she wished she could see his.

"I have date palms that shade the patios. The fruit is used in the kitchen. For color there's red bougainvillea, white oleander and a large variety of roses. My mother's always bringing me new rosebushes. They're her passion. Her own garden is so overrun with them, she has to foist new plants on me."

She fell quiet at the mention of his mother. All the doubts returned.

"You'll like my home, Chloe," he said gently.

Twelve

Her eyes flew to his in the erratic light from other cars. "Do you have pictures you could show me?" she asked.

"You'll have to wait until we get there to see it."

"I'm not going there," she said hastily.

"You and Mackenzie can come for a short visit," he returned easily, his tight jaw the only indication his mood was not as serene as his voice indicated.

The limo stopped before the portico of the Williams Hotel. Salid opened the rear door, permitting Karif and Chloe to climb out.

She should have been firmer when she'd told him she had no intention of visiting his home.

When the elevator doors opened and revealed an empty car, Karif shook his head at Salid and entered alone with Chloe. Pushing the button for his floor, Karif then turned to her and cupped her face with his warm palms.

"Did you enjoy the symphony, *chérie?*" he asked, gazing down at her.

"Yes, it was wonderful."

Looking into his dark eyes, she felt as if she'd plunged into a magical midnight. As he lowered his head she couldn't move. Slowly her eyes closed and she parted her lips for his kiss.

Liquid heat poured through her. His touch provoked a storm of sensations. The soft caressing strokes of his thumbs against her cheeks sparked shivers of excitement, while the magic of his kiss drove all coherent thought from her mind.

For the moment, Chloe could only exist to kiss and be kissed. Her only reality was his touch. Her only tie to earth was his mouth and his hands. She was floating, reveling in the long-forgotten delight of being kissed by Karif.

The ding of the elevator announced the floor. Silently, the doors parted. Time stood still. Then he pulled back, slowly, reluctantly. Gazing down at her damp lips, he brushed his thumb across them once. Chloe trembled at the sensuous caress, not caring that her heart was in her eyes. Not caring for anything but being back in Karif's arms.

"Come, supper awaits." He released her and guided her to his suite, nodding in passing at the men who stood on duty by his door.

Chloe avoided their eyes, knowing they must have witnessed the kiss when the elevator doors opened. For a moment she had felt so special, but seeing the guards reminded her of the notation in Paul's preliminary report. Karif was used to escorting beautiful women around London and Paris.

Was she being added to the list for his stay in Washington? Did he invite them all back to Manasia to see his home by the sea?

The guards were probably used to seeing him bring women back to his suite at midnight. She didn't want to be just another woman in his life. She'd rather have had it all end ten years ago than be one in a long line.

"I need to get home," she said, stopping just inside the door.

He cocked an eyebrow. "Why now?"

"It's late. I'm not hungry. I need to go home," she repeated. She refused to meet his eyes.

She knew her own limitations. She was too susceptible to his charm. When she was with him, she had a hard time remembering what had happened in the past.

Being with him felt right. She was tempted to give in to the longing to throw caution to the winds and accept whatever he had in mind.

But her sense of self-protection flared. She had to protect her heart.

"I had a special dinner prepared for us. Stay and enjoy it and then I'll take you home," Karif said as he crossed the room to the table set exquisitely beneath the large window that overlooked Washington. Tall tapers burned, illuminating the table and the immediate area. The rest of the room was shadowed, with only discreet lighting here and there to relieve the darkness. Soft music filtered through. The setting was romantic—seductive almost.

Slowly Chloe walked to the table, feeling as if she were in a dream. No one had ever set the stage for seduction for her.

The pristine white cloth that covered the table was set with china, silver and crystal. A low arrangement of roses sat in the center, their heady fragrance permeating the air, adding to the dreamlike atmosphere. She glanced at Karif but he was busy uncorking the champagne that had been resting in a silver ice bucket.

The pop startled her. Wiping suddenly damp palms against her dress, she felt wrapped in silken bonds. She felt special, worthy of such attention, thrilled that Karif had seen to such an exquisite dinner.

No matter that he'd probably done this a dozen times before--it had never happened to her and she was flattered.

And wary. What did he expect from her?

"To us, Chloe." He handed her a flute of icy champagne and touched the edge of his glass to hers. Sipping the sparkling wine, his eyes never left hers.

Chloe sipped. *To us?*

There was no us. In truth, there never had been. Without honesty relationships withered and died.

Yet she'd loved him. Had longed for an *us*.

She looked away before Karif saw something in her eyes that she refused to admit to herself.

Karif noticed the slight trembling of her fingers and a feeling of hope pervaded. She wasn't as immune to the attraction between them as she pretended. He reached for her glass taking it from her fingers and putting it on the table.

Leaning over, he brushed his lips against hers. Pausing to lightly probe the dark warmth of her mouth, he could taste the champagne and the sweet taste that was her own.

"Sit and enjoy dinner, *chérie*," he said, guiding her to a chair, seating her.

He sat opposite her and studied her as one of the waiters responded to his signal entered and served them. She looked lovely. The candlelight enhanced her beauty. Her brown eyes were a mixture of shyness and uncertainty. For a moment, he thought he'd glimpsed something more, but wasn't sure.

In fact, he wasn't sure about her at all. And that made him edgy. He was used to being obeyed instantly. She fought him every step of the way. He knew why. She felt betrayed. He should have done more to find her ten years before.

At the time he'd thought he'd done all possible. If he had suspected his father's interference, he'd have taken different steps.

Nothing could change the past. Now he had to find a way to make her listen to him, to open herself up to the possibilities that lay before them.

He thought about Mackenzie. He felt a warm glow near his heart whenever he thought about his daughter. He wanted to get to know her, have her know him. Love him.

How ironic that his father had never known about Mackenzie. He'd have loved a granddaughter. His mother would be pleased. She'd been surrounded by males all her married life. She would delight in a granddaughter and probably spoil her to bits.

He smiled at the thought. His mother would love Mackenzie. And Chloe.

"Tell me where you went, what you did after you left Berkeley," Karif said when the waiter left. He wanted to learn all he could about her. Discover what had forged her into the woman she was today.

Glad for the opportunity to end the awkward silence Chloe complied. She told him how she'd first done freelance photography to earn enough money to keep herself and the baby. Then as Mackenzie had grown older, how she had found work on one of the Los Angeles papers.

"Then I had a break. I happened to be at the right place at the right time when L.A. had those mudslides that killed so many. I got right into the situation and my pictures were picked up by AP and UPI. That led to the offer from the *Sentinel* and so I came to Washington. I've worked hard and it's payed off. Now I get to cover the White House."

Karif watched her as she spoke. She loved her work, that was obvious. Her eyes shone, her voice was animated, and her expression was one of contented happiness. Confidence in her ability came through. Gone was the sassy college student he'd once known. In her place was a beautiful, successful woman. Strong and courageous, she still possessed that delicate femininity than he remembered.

"And you like Washington."

"Very much. I can't imagine living anywhere else."

"Except Manasia," he said smoothly.

She blinked. "I'm not going there."

"You haven't even seen my country. You can come for a visit. If you don't like it, we will have to see what other arrangements we can make."

"Karif, stop. You talk like it's a done deal. I'm not going anywhere with you. Especially to your home."

He filled her glass again, ignoring her protests He wasn't getting into an argument this evening. If she'd just give it a chance, she'd love it. Its beauty would appeal to her artistic side. She would not regret leaving Washington. And they could visit often.

"Are you listening to me?" she asked sharply.

He smiled and shook his head. "I'm only hearing what I want tonight. It's been a perfect evening, I'm not spoiling it by fighting."

She was even beautiful when she was angry. The color flying in her cheeks deepened, her eyes sparkled.

"Though, perhaps I can change your mind about visiting if I tell you more," he said as she glared at him.

"I doubt it," Chloe muttered.

"Listen and see," Karif said, smiling at her frowning face. He then began to paint pictures in her mind of the high desert, the lonely stretches of land that swept the far horizons. The beauty in the lush temperate area near the Mediterranean, the lofty peaks of the distant mountains.

He spoke of star-studded skies, like black velvet with a million sparkling diamonds, the air so clear a person felt as if he could touch them.

He spoke of a warm and struggling people, anxious to enjoy the benefits of modern western life while clinging to traditions and customs. Of the ancient cities blending with modern high rises.

And he told her about his family. Of his mother, who'd be thrilled to learn she had a granddaughter and anxious to meet her. Of his brothers and their families-- cousins for Mackenzie to play with. Aunts and uncles with whom to share their culture and history.

Chloe listened and despite her attempts to remain firm she was fascinated. She'd love to see Manasia with Karif.

She could imagine the sweep of desert dunes, almost feel the clean dry air rushing by if they went riding on the purebred Arabian horses he mentioned. She'd love to swim in the Mediterranean, see the roses his mother planted, explore the souks and Casbahs of the old cities.

"Come for a visit, Chloe," he urged.

She stopped for a moment to truly consider it. It would be a wonderful vacation. And she could see where he lived, how he lived.

Then reality intruded. She shook her head. "I can't. I have a job and there's Mackenzie."

"I can take care of you and Mackenzie. Quit your job, come with me," he urged.

"No!" Chloe pushed back her chair and stood. Karif was too persuasive. She had to leave before she did something she'd regret.

"I will not be seduced to do what you want. This elaborate setting notwithstanding, I won't go to Manasia with you. I'm going home. And I'm staying there."

She turned toward the door but had taken only two steps before his hands caught her shoulders and spun her around to face him.

"You think I'm seducing you to fall in with my wishes? Maybe we're not too far apart, after all, *chérie*," he said. "Stay the night."

She shook her head. "Not happening. I'm going home. I can get a cab." She tilted her chin, meeting his gaze squarely, determination shining from hers.

He lowered his face and kissed her cheek.

"No!" she said hotly, turning away, afraid of the traitorous feelings that began to curl through her.

He ignored her and brushed his lips across her jaw.

Involuntarily, Chloe arched her neck, offering him better access to her throat.

Karif accepted her invitation, his mouth moving against the delicate skin until his lips rested on the pulse at the base of her throat. He lifted his head only enough to find her mouth and capture it with his own.

He kissed her until her senses spun. Until Chloe lost her rigid posture and stepped closer to his embrace. His hands moved to bring her against him, causing shivers of delight as he caressed her shoulders. The soft silk permitted the heat of his hands to warm her as sensations of delight swept through.

"Make no mistake, *cherie,* this discussion is not over," Karif said against her lips before he eased back. His dark eyes glittered down at her. "Come, I will take you home."

Chloe moved as if in a trance. Her blood sang in her veins. Her heart pounded so loud, she was sure he could hear it--the guards in the hall probably heard it.

Slowly she walked to the door, feeling confused. His touch was potent, his charm more than she could resist. Yet she knew she had to. The past had shown her what the future would hold. He'd never mentioned love. She knew without it they had nothing.

When the limousine pulled away from the hotel, Karif flipped the switch that slid the connecting window closed. They were cocooned in a dark world of their own. He pulled Chloe into his lap and kissed her before she could think of resisting. His hands were against her throat, threading into her soft hair, moving over her arm, over her hip. She caught her breath as his palm gently rubbed against her, his touch penetrating through the material as if it weren't there. She felt the old familiar heat building, the desire for closeness warring with the need for sanity.

"No," she said, shaking her head, her lips hovering near his. She couldn't let the madness take hold. She had to draw the line.

But she ached with longing.

He linked his fingers with hers. Her lips kissed. Her tongue darted out, danced with his, invited back. Her breathing mingled with his. Her heart beat in unison with his.

When the limo stopped in front of her house, it was several minutes before either realized it. Gradually, awareness seeped into Chloe's mind. She lifted her head, tried to see Karif's eyes, but it was too dark.

Karif set her beside him and flipped on a small light. "You look thoroughly kissed," he said with blatant satisfaction.

"I feel thoroughly kissed," she murmured, loath to leave, knowing she had to.

"I'll call in the morning," he said. "I told Mackenzie I'd take her anywhere she wanted. Will you come with us? You two decide what we can do and tell me when I call."

Numb, Chloe nodded.

Karif flipped off the light and lowered the connecting window. In only seconds Salid had the door open. Karif escorted Chloe to her door and bade her a quick goodnight.

Despite the lateness of the hour, Chloe couldn't sleep. She prepared for bed, climbed in and lay wide awake.

She was totally confused.

She became more attracted to Karif every time she saw him. She'd been thrilled listening to him talk of his country. Would they have had a different outcome if his father hadn't intervened?

She was flattered beyond belief at the attention he paid her. And she was tempted to give in to the invitation to visit.

Yet she still didn't trust her judgement. Nothing gave her enough confidence to let her heart rule her head.

She'd done that once before and the results had been disastrous. She dared not risk it again. She was older now and wiser. This time her head would rule.

On the other hand Chloe was very much afraid she was falling in love all over again. Chloe tried to argue herself out of it. Karif talked of wanting her in his life, but had he also wanted those women whose names Paul had in his preliminary report?

Karif had married. That hurt most of all.

She hadn't dated other men beyond having a fun time. He'd married another woman and had she not tragically died, he'd still be married to her.

Above all was Mackenzie. Was he trying to capture her daughter's heart? Was his attention only about that?

Chloe rolled over and pulled a pillow over her head as if that would block out her thoughts. She couldn't stand it if he only wanted to be with her because of Mackenzie.

Not when she wanted him so much for himself.

Thirteen

Chloe awoke the next morning to the faint drone of the television and the wonderful aroma of fresh coffee. Mrs. Hanson had stayed the night as she did whenever Chloe had to be out late. She'd obviously prepared breakfast.

Stretching, Chloe rolled over on the bed thinking about the previous evening.

In retrospect, it seemed like a dream. The wonderful music at the Kennedy Center, meeting and talking with some of the nation's most distinguished men, the candle-lit supper with the beauty of the Washington night visible from the table. It had been the most romantic evening she'd ever spent.

Karif's kisses had added to the romance. Though she knew he'd wanted more, he brought her home safe and sound. Or was he honoring her requests because he wanted to please her? She didn't have a clue.

For this morning at least, she'd revel in the sweet memories of the evening.

Her door cracked open and Mackenzie peeked in. Smiling when she saw her mother awake, she bounded in and hopped up on the bed then snuggling down beside

Chloe.

"I didn't think you were ever going to wake up, Mom," she said. "Mrs. Hanson's going to fix pancakes as soon as you get up. I'm starving."

"Starving, huh? Poor waif child." Chloe tickled her, delighting in her childish laughter.

"Did you have a good time last night?" Mackenzie asked a minute later, her eyes watchful.

Chloe smiled at her daughter. "Yes. It was very nice."

What an understatement. *Nice* was not the word to describe the evening. *Special, spectacular, magical,* those would all be better words.

Mackenzie wrinkled her nose. "All you did was sit and listen to slow music. They didn't even have a video, I bet," she said.

"No, no videos, but the music was lovely and after the concert we went back to Karif's hotel and had a late supper. With chocolate mousse for dessert."

With a pang, Chloe realized her abrupt departure had meant she'd left before she'd had a chance to eat hers. It had looked lovely.

"Did you bring some home for me?" Mackenzie asked hopefully.

Chloe chuckled and drew her closer. "No, pumpkin."

"How come you and my father don't live together like Stephie's parents?" Mackenzie asked.

Chloe's heart lurched. She'd been waiting for the right moment to sit down with Mackenzie and discuss the situation more fully. Somehow the perfect time hadn't arrived. She should have been the one to bring up the situation and explain it to Mackenzie. Only, she wasn't sure how she'd explain everything.

"For one thing, Karif lives far away from Washington. So we can't live together."

"But he lived in Berkeley when you did. You were talking about it at dinner the other night. If he lived in the United States then, why did he leave?"

"He had to go home because his father was very sick and needed him at home."

Chloe was not going to tell Mackenzie how Karif's father had done all in his considerable power to keep his son from the American woman he felt would be wrong for him.

"Why didn't you go with him?"

"I didn't know where he went. He left very suddenly without telling anyone where he was going."

The old anguish flared, though it had lost some of its potency. Maybe he had tried to find her--maybe it was fate that kept them apart.

Though she wasn't sure she could forgive the fact that he'd kept so many important parts of his identity a secret. She'd shared everything--and he had only told her bits and pieces--nothing of major importance.

"And he didn't ever come back to see you?" Mackenzie asked.

"Well, I had to move away from Berkeley to get a good job, so I wasn't there when Karif tried to find me. Remember our apartment in L.A. before we moved here?"

Mackenzie nodded and remained silent for a long time. Chloe drew a deep breath.

"What should I call him?" Mackenzie asked.

"Who? Karif?"

Mackenzie nodded. "Stephie calls her father Daddy. Should I call him Daddy?"

Chloe was at a loss. What *should* her daughter call her father? Closing her eyes, she wished the entire situation would vanish. She didn't like being in this position. She didn't want Mackenzie and Karif to build a closeness that would exclude her. She didn't want her daughter to rely on him when she was all Chloe had.

"Mom?"

"I don't know what you should call him. Ask him when you see him." Chloe knew Karif was planning to see Mackenzie today. He could answer her questions.

Somehow, she couldn't picture him as a daddy. Yet father seemed too formal.

"Okay," Mackenzie said. "Maybe he'll want to be called Daddy. I think I like having a daddy."

Chloe nodded. "He said he's going to call this morning to see what you want to do today."

Chloe was thankful that the question of what to call Karif was uppermost in Mackenzie's mind and not all the other convoluted facts of their dilemma. If only things were as simple for her.

"I know. He told me. I want to go to Air and Space."

"You always want to go to Air and Space," Chloe said with a smile.

"But I love it. And you like it, too, don't you, Mom?"

"Yes, but we were just there a couple of months ago."

"Yeah, but I bet *he* wasn't. Maybe he's never been there."

"We'll see. Now, how about those pancakes Mrs.

Hanson is going to fix us?" Chloe asked. "I think I'm starving, too."

Mackenzie giggled and flung herself from the bed and out the door. "I get the first batch," she called as she raced down the hall.

A typical Saturday morning, Chloe thought as she left the bed more slowly than she did on weekdays. Well, not typical, maybe. It wasn't often she had someone else prepare breakfast. What a treat.

They finished breakfast and lingered around the table. Mrs. Hanson questioned Chloe about her evening, enjoying hearing about the Kennedy Center, the music and the late-night supper.

In turn, she and Mackenzie let Chloe know how difficult it had been to complete the jigsaw puzzle.

The phone rang.

"I'll get it." Mackenzie pushed back her chair and ran to the phone on the kitchen wall.

"Hello?... Yes... Yes... Mom said you'd call..."

Chloe felt her nerves stretch to the breaking point. It was Karif.

"Air and Space....it's really cool. There're old airplanes and spaceships, real ones, and hot-air balloons." She listened for a moment and then turned to her mother.

"Mom, you're going with us, aren't you?"

Chloe nodded far more calmly than she felt.

"Yes, she's going. What time do we have to be ready? Um, you know you don't have to wear a suit to Air and Space?"

Chloe's lips twitched. She wondered what Karif thought of his daughter's kindly letting him know what would be suitable attire for the museum. She wished she could see his face right now.

"Okay, we'll be ready at ten."

Mackenzie hung up as Chloe glanced at the clock. It was already after nine. She stood, gathered the dishes and carried them to the sink.

"I'll do those. Sounds like you and Mackenzie have to get ready to leave before long," Mrs. Hanson said as she, too, gathered dirty dishes.

"No, I have time to do them. After cooking that wonderful breakfast, the last thing you need to do is clean up. Relax, have another cup of coffee. We have plenty of time to get ready. Right, Mackenzie?"

Promptly at ten the limo pulled up in front of Chloe's house. She opened the door to greet Karif, Mackenzie hanging back a little.

"Good morning," Karif said, leaning over to kiss Chloe as if he had been doing it for years.

Too surprised to move, Chloe felt his lips brush against hers. Lightly, affectionately, nothing earth-shattering--even though she felt it in every cell of her body. He straightened and looked at Mackenzie, his face softening into a smile.' "And good morning to you, *petite*."

"Hi." Mackenzie was shy, watching Karif warily.

"If we can take your car, I'll let the limo go. Your car will give us a bit of anonymity," he said.

"That's fine." Chloe said. What did the problems with finding a parking place have to do with anything? If he wanted her to drive, after that kiss she would agree to almost anything.

"Salid not coming?" Chloe asked as she watched the

limo drive away.

"I think I can manage on my own for one day," Karif said dryly.

"You're the one who told me he went with you everywhere, that it was his job to accompany the sheikh."

"Ah, but today I'm going incognito. So I certainly don't want him tagging along to give rise to questions."

Incognito--as he'd lived in Berkeley.

What other secrets was he still keeping ?

To him it was a lark, a way to escape his normal life. To her it had been a betrayal of all her feelings. She'd shared everything and he had shared virtually nothing.

"Now what erected that wall?" Karif asked.

"What do you mean?"

"Every so often I feel you softening toward me, and then immediately you erect an impenetrable barrier. What caused this one?"

"I don't know what you mean. I'll just get my purse and we'll be ready to go. Oh, Mackenzie has a question for you."

She felt as if she were throwing her daughter to the wolves, but she didn't want to pursue Karif's line of questioning.

Today she was going to do her best to keep the bitterness away. The past was over. It was up to her to make the most of the present—for Mackenzie's sake.

"And what is that, *petite?*" Karif stooped until he was at eye level with Mackenzie.

He knew she was shy around him. He wanted to hug her and tell her she meant the world to him but knew enough about children to know that'd be a totally wrong approach. He'd likely scare her half to death. He needed to tread carefully until she was comfortable around him. He was enchanted with his daughter--he'd do nothing to harm their budding relationship.

"I didn't know what to call you. I asked Mom but she said I had to ask you," Mackenzie said, her eyes on the top button of his casual shirt.

"Ah, that is something we have to decide, isn't it? Let's see. I called my father Father. What do you think?"

"My friend Stephie calls her father Daddy," Mackenzie said, raising her eyes as far as his chin.

"That's very American," Karif commented, feeling a small clutch in his heart at the term.

"Mackenzie is American," Chloe said, standing near them.

Karif met her eyes--was there a challenge there? He stood slowly, his gaze locked with hers. "Of course, but she is also Manasian. How nice to have dual citizenship."

"Mackenzie, run along to the bathroom. It'll be hours before we're home again," Chloe said, longing to break eye contact, mesmerized by the compelling gaze locked with hers.

"But we haven't decided," she protested.

"I think Daddy would be fine," Karif said.

"Okay." She scampered down the hall.

The tension in the entryway rose as Karif took a step closer to Chloe. "And do you approve of her calling me Daddy?"

"I don't seem to have much choice in the matter. You made sure of that," Chloe said.

"You wanted me to lie and say I was not her father?"

"She never suspected. You pushed and pushed until I had no choice but to tell her."

"Yes, you're correct. And I'd do it again. She *is* my daughter. You should have told me when you first saw me."

"Well, there're probably a lot of things I should have done in my life and haven't. This isn't the only one," she snapped.

He stepped closer, giving in to the almost compulsive urge to tangle his fingers in her silky hair. The warmth of her skin enveloped him as he drew her closer. Her eyes were wide and wary, her body resistant. But she'd never been indifferent to his touch. Nothing had changed. From the first time he'd seen her so long ago she'd inflamed his senses. She still did.

Slowly he lowered his mouth to hers. His lips coaxed. Slowly, she gave in, relaxing in his embrace, responding to the heat of his kiss.

"I'm read—" Mackenzie stopped dead.

Karif lifted his head and smiled at the bemused expression on Chloe's face. "Good. We are ready, as well. Shall I drive?"

"No. I know my way around Washington and it's my car. I'll drive."

Chloe needed something to stop her rioting senses. Focusing on driving in D.C. would do the trick. Maybe accompanying them on this outing wasn't the best idea after all.

Or maybe she should attempt to enjoy herself.

Once among the crowd in the museum she'd regain her equilibrium. She held on to that thought as she maneuvered through the Saturday traffic, conscious every second of Karif sitting only inches away.

They waited in line to clear the checkpoint, then entered the vast lobby of the National Air and Space Museum. Above them hung various airplanes of different sizes, configurations and colors.

"Which one flew across the ocean?" Mackenzie asked, her eyes gazing with rapture at the suspended planes.

"That one." Chloe pointed out the Spirit of St. Louis.

"Isn't this cool, Daddy?" the little girl asked, moving to stand a bit nearer Karif.

Chloe glanced at Karif to see how he was taking the quick adoption of Mackenzie calling him Daddy. He was smiling at his daughter.

"This is magnificent. This was an excellent choice."

"Have you been here before?" Mackenzie asked.

"No. This is my first visit to Washington and I have been tied up in meetings for most of the time. I'm glad we came here today," he replied.

Someone bumped Chloe and she stepped out of their way. The Air and Space Museum was always crowded but especially on weekends. She moved closer to Karif to insure she didn't get separated and he reached out and drew her against him, his arm around her waist.

She glanced up at him from beneath her lashes, her heart pounding. Did he realize just touching her drove every prudent thought from her mind? She wanted to lean against him, pretend everything was the way she once thought it would be. Knowing she couldn't dislodge his hold without causing a scene, she relaxed enough to allow herself to enjoy his touch, imprinting the feel against her so she could bring forth the memories to cherish in the years to come.

They walked around the first floor, stopping to study different aircraft, reading the plaques that explained their history. The noise level was steady as patrons exclaimed over spaceships and gliders, satellites and hot-air balloons.

Gradually the butterflies in her stomach settled down and Chloe was able to enjoy the different exhibits even though Karif's touch kept her on the edge.

Once when Mackenzie turned back to share her delight in an exhibit, Chloe's breath caught. For this day at least, they were a family— mother, father, child. The bittersweet sensation that rushed through startled her.

If things had been different this might be a normal activity for them. They'd go places together, share in their enjoyment of the different things they saw, their delight in being together.

Karif focused on Mackenzie. He listened to her when she shared her views of the different exhibits, answered questions she raised, and kept an eye on her to make sure she didn't get lost in the crowd.

He never stopped touching Chloe. When they paused to read a plaque, he'd rest his hands on her shoulders, lowering his head near hers, reading over her shoulder. Sometimes he pulled her back against his chest as they studied the various exhibits.

When they walked, his hand gently encircled her as if to keep her close. At one point, he rubbed his fingertips lightly against her waist commenting that she was too thin.

It took all her concentration to keep from flinging

herself against him and demanding that he make hot love to her.

Yet she cherished every second. She'd never thought to feel this away again--not after the barren existence she'd led this past decade. She wished every moment could last for eternity. Wished things would never change and that they could wander through the museum forever, Karif's hands on her. Sharing the day with the daughter they'd created.

"I'm hungry," Mackenzie said.

Chloe glanced at her watch, it was after one.

"I guess you are, pumpkin, it's past your normal lunchtime."

"And where would you like to eat?" Karif asked.

"The cafeteria," Mackenzie said instantly.

He was puzzled.

"It's the cafeteria for Air and Space and has fast food places that kids love." Chloe explained.

"If Mackenzie wishes it, then let's eat there. This day's for her."

Chloe nodded and turned to head for the cafeteria--a bit of her enjoyment gone.

This was all for Mackenzie. What had she expected?

If she thought about it, most of the contact between them had been for Mackenzie, if not directly, then as a means for Karif to get to know her.

The cafeteria was jammed. The noise level rose with so many families talking, eating, laughing, enjoying themselves. Spying a couple just leaving, Chloe dashed over to claim the small table. Karif held Mackenzie's hand as they followed.

"What would you like, they have everything!" Mackenzie said, her face alight with pleasure.

Karif studied the large menus hanging one one wall. Hamburgers, french fries, pizzas--it looked like a kid's delight.

Chloe took out her wallet and withdrew some bills. "You can have what you want, I'll get them. You sit here and save the table."

"Do not be insulting, *cherie*, I'll take care of the meal."

She hesitated, then nodded. She hoped he wasn't put off by the fast foods.

In a short time they were oblivious to the crowd around them as they ate their lunch with relish. Chloe was amused to see Karif had chosen pizza.

"Comparing to La Val's?" she asked.

He nodded calmly. "I think I shall make it as scientific as possible. Maybe while I'm in America, I can test a dozen or more and render a decision."

She giggled, picturing the aloof sheikh going from pizza parlor to pizza parlor sampling each to determine the best.

"Ice cream for dessert," Mackenzie said as she wiped a napkin across her mouth. "In waffle cones."

Karif raised an eyebrow at the comment and looked across the small table to Chloe.

"I'll have chocolate," she said, smiling.

As Chloe watched as the two threaded their way through the crowded floor her smile faded. Karif held his daughter's hand leaning over slightly to hear what Mackenzie was saying. Chloe's heart was touched. They looked natural together. The entire day was special, like a moment out of time. Something she'd never envisioned in all the years she'd had Mackenzie.

Chloe continued to watch as they wound their way back. Karif held two cones in one hand, his other firmly wrapped around Mackenzie's, keeping her close.

He'd be a wonderful father, Chloe acknowledged. He'd love his children, shower them with attention and yet she suspected he'd make sure they received the proper discipline to grow into worthy adults.

Tears blurred her vision as she looked away blinking furiously. She'd wanted him to be the father of her children. Why had fate intervened?

Karif handed Chloe her cone, noticing the spiky lashes.

"Did something happen?" he asked, concerned as he discerned the tears still shimmering in her eyes. Had something hurt her?

Instantly, he scanned the area.

She shook her head and delicately licked her cone, blinking a couple more times. She felt embarrassed he'd noticed her tears.

"Maybe after we're finished eating you would like to browse the gift shop," she said quickly.

"Mom always brings me a present if she has to go away on a trip. Are you going to take your mom a present?" Mackenzie asked.

"I think that'd be a good idea, Mackenzie. You can help me pick it out."

"What's she like? Your mom?" Mackenzie asked shyly.

Karif studied his daughter. His mother was her

grandmother.

He hadn't really thought much about what finding Chloe and Mackenzie would do to his family. He'd been so astounded at the fact that he was a father, he hadn't thought about how the rest of his family would react.

They would be surprised—that was for sure.

But pleased, he thought.

"I tell you what. When we get back to your house, we'll Skype her. It'll be late at home but I think she'll still be up. She's a nice lady. Not too tall. She still has very dark hair. She loves children. She has three grandsons, but you're her only granddaughter."

Mackenzie smiled at him then at her mother. "I never had a grandmother before."

"You also have three uncles, two aunts and three cousins. On my side, that is."

He remembered Chloe had said she was an only child. Were her parents still alive? They hadn't spent much time talking about their families. In Berkeley he'd deliberately steered their conversations away from their personal lives, trying to keep his identity secret.

Now he wished he'd handled things differently. He should have told Chloe the truth. Would it have made a difference in the long run? He believed so. She would have known how to contact him for one thing.

"You don't have grandparents on your mother's side?" Karif asked.

Mackenzie was an open forthright child. He felt totally at ease talking with her. There was none of the awkwardness he'd anticipated. Was this a normal father-daughter bond?

"My mother died before I went to college," Chloe offered.

"But she has a grandfather, your father."

Mackenzie shook her head. "He doesn't love my mom anymore. He said he didn't want her anymore. Mom and I both don't have a dad. Oh!" She looked stricken as she stared up at Karif. "Now I guess I have one."

"Yes, you do. I didn't know about you, Mackenzie, or I would have come to see you before now."

He could already feel the tendrils of love circling his heart for this adorable child. Some of it was because of her resemblance to her mother. Her voice and mannerisms mimicked Chloe's.

Yet Mackenzie was a person in her own right, and he was intrigued to discover all there was to find out about this child he'd created and not known about.

Fourteen

When they finished their ice cream cones, they left the crowded cafeteria and returned to Air and Space to visit the gift shop.

Both Mackenzie and Karif were intrigued with the different children's books explaining space travel, aerodynamics and the history of zeppelins. He bought her one book on the story of Charles Lindbergh and his flight across the Atlantic.

"Thank you, Daddy," she said when he handed her the bag containing the book.

"You're most welcome," he replied. Looking at Chloe, he said, "You've done a fine job raising our daughter, *cherie*. She isn't at all greedy and has nice manners."

Chloe felt the compliment warm her heart. Life had been so difficult at times. She was touched he was pleased with what she'd done.

He looked at Mackenzie again. "Are you getting tired?" he said, noticing the bounce she'd shown that morning was missing.

"No," she said quickly.

He laughed, remembering when as a boy he never

wanted to stop even when he was tired beyond measure. "Maybe just a little bit?"

She shrugged, holding her bag in both hands.

"How about we go watch the movie in the Imax, that'll give me time to rest. This museum is amazing, but with so much to see, my head's spinning," Karif said.

"Okay." She offered her hand and he took it in his, touched she was warming up to him so quickly.

Chloe followed them to the theater unsure how she felt that Mackenzie was becoming more at ease with Karif.

He looked at her when she joined them. Her gaze was on Mackenzie, her expression difficult to read, but he knew it wasn't the same carefree happiness he'd seen earlier.

She was erecting barriers again. Why she was so unwilling to give them a chance?

Granted, she'd gone through a lot all alone. Things had changed. Hadn't he made it clear he wanted them to be a couple again?

Yet she continued to resist.

If he had to fight her every inch of the way, one day he hoped she'd realize that they belonged together. His daughter deserved a chance to have both parents raise her. He deserved the opportunity to know his daughter and to contribute to her life.

He wanted to change Chloe's life, as well, to make up for the difficulties she'd faced for so long. She'd live like a princess in Manasia. She wouldn't have to work if she didn't wish.

He was certain she'd love his country.

And if she wanted to help him, that would be a huge

asset. There was much to do to continue Manasia's economic progress.

If not, she could simply be his refuge when the demands of running the country became too great.

He remembered the days of laughter and heated discussion they'd shared in Berkeley. The dark nights when they'd walk and talk long after the shops had closed and most people were home. He'd cherished those times with Chloe, feeling closer to her than anyone else in his life.

Over the last ten years, he'd missed those times almost unbearably. Could he ever recapture that warmth and acceptance? Could she find it in her to forgive him the deceptions?

Forgive him for not finding her when she needed him so much?

One way or another, he hoped she would. He couldn't let her go a second time.

The big theater was almost full when they found seats near the left side mid way down. Mackenzie led the way in, followed by Karif and then Chloe.

When they were seated, he took her hand and threaded his fingers with hers. "I'm glad to be sitting for a while."

She nodded, acutely aware of their fingers entwined. "I know, if I had her energy I'd hold up better."

He started to say something just as the movie was beginning, so they both settled back to watch the film.

He absently rubbed his thumb over the back of her hand. Today was turning out to be almost perfect.

Chloe was glad to have to concentrate on the traffic

when it was time go home. She needed something to take her mind off Karif. She didn't know if she dared let herself trust him again.

She did know she was still attracted to him. She longed for his kisses. She remembered when they'd been as close as two people could ever be. Her spirit wanted that again. Her body yearned for that closeness. His kisses filled her with bliss.

If she dared reach out for the happiness that teased her, would she find it, or find it all an illusion?

Mackenzie ran to the answering machine when they reached home. The blinking light indicated a message. She listened to the message and turned to her mother.

"It's Stephie. She wants to know if I can go swimming. Can I, Mom?" she asked as Chloe and Karif settled the various packages on the coffee table in the living room.

"Yes, be back for dinner."

"Cool."

Chloe smiled as she heard Mackenzie call her friend, then run down the hall to change into her swimsuit.

"I'm tired after all that walking. And she seems to have as much energy as if she'd just gotten up," Chloe said as she sank onto the sofa and eased her shoes off.

Karif sat beside her, leaning his head against the high back. "I have thought for many years that energy is wasted on the young. My nephews never seem to run down."

"Tell me about them," Chloe said, wanting to learn more about him.

"Let's see," he closed his eyes. "Hamid is the oldest. He's my next brother's child. At five, he's inquisitive and into everything. His parents taught him how to swim at a young age since he was forever plunging into the sea without a bit of concern."

For the next few minutes Karif talked about his brothers and their wives and the three nephews who obviously enjoyed his deep love.

"But you'll see when you get there how bright they are. Hamid even speaks English. Not as well as he will one day but enough to communicate. Mackenzie'll have no problems with communication."

"You're going too fast, Karif. We're not going to Manasia," Chloe said, the bubble bursting.

He opened his eyes a slit and looked at her.

"It's not too fast, *cherie*. I have a lot of years to make up. I want you both to come. One way or the other. Actually, I'm hoping you'll come as my wife."

Wife!

She held her breath, her gaze locking with his. Was he serious? He truly wanted to marry her?

She dropped her gaze to her lap. One fingernail had broken and she worried the ragged edge while she tried desperately to think. Ten years ago she'd thought they'd get married after college. Back then she'd wanted it more than anything.

Now--she wasn't sure.

Karif watched her sensing the nervous energy that was building.

He reached out and covered her restless fingers with his. He'd hoped she'd throw her arms around him and accept immediately.

Cynically he reflected he should have known better.

She hadn't exactly thrown herself at him once during the past few days.

Now she looked as if she were thinking up a polite way to tell him to get lost.

"I haven't asked you, so don't build walls and barriers. I'll ask before I have to leave the country, however, so you think long and hard about it. I want you back in my life, Chloe. And I want my daughter to be a part of my life. Marriage would simplify things. But if you want to do things the hard way, I'll deal with that, as well."

"Well, that certainly is a romantic way to look at things."

She flung off his hands and stood pacing across the room. Pausing only a moment at the window, she turned and walked back toward the fireplace.

The phone rang and Karif could see the relief on her face. She answered it and from her side of the conversation it sounded as if she'd been invited somewhere.

Briefly jealousy touched him. For years he'd assumed she had gone on with her life, had married and started a family. Gradually, he'd accepted that.

But the reality that she hadn't now made it imperative that she not consider anyone but him.

He rose as she clicked off.

"Who was that?"

She looked surprised that he would ask.

"The Andersons, Stephie's parents. They invited us to come swimming, too. I said no."

Karif studied her. Was she thinking about his comment regarding marriage? Was she going to be difficult about it when the time came?

He'd ask her in a heartbeat but knew she'd refuse today. Given enough time, he was counting on her accepting.

"It's one thing to go in crowds where no one knows us, but I don't want neighbors getting the wrong idea," she blurted out, watching him warily.

"Wrong idea?" His voice was silky in its tone.

He was at his most formidable when using that tone.

Chloe shivered and shrugged trying to dispel the sense of impending doom.

"They'd want to know all about you and I don't need that now. You're leaving soon. There'd be too much talk about Mackenzie. I want to protect her."

"And you think she won't be talking about me with her friend Stephie?" he asked.

Chloe shrugged.

"In other words, you have no intention of marrying me. You've made up your mind that you want nothing to do with me. You don't want anyone to know that Mackenzie is my daughter, is that it?"

"That's it," she said, raising to face him. "You say you want something more from me, but it's early days yet. I've had proof of your staying power, it's totally lacking. I'm not risking my daughter."

"You're not risking your *heart, chérie*. Your daughter's the wall you use to hide behind. It's not Mackenzie we're discussing, but you and me."

"Okay, then, you're right! I don't trust you."

"So what must I do to provide you with enough trust to at least think of a future together?"

"I don't know."

She blinked back tears she refused to let fall. She wanted to believe in him. Yet he'd never said a word of love.

She wanted to trust that he'd never lie to her again, never leave her alone--but she didn't. What would convince her?

"Time, I guess," she said, biting down on her lower lip to keep it from trembling.

"Time." He sighed softly and leaned forward his lips touching hers, coaxing a response. Slowly he drew her to him deepening the kiss.

Doubts fled when he held her like this. Fears and uncertainty melted as the heat they generated burned up every doubt, everything but the fiery love that blossomed each time he touched her.

She loved Karif. She had always loved him. She undoubtably always would love him.

If only she was brave enough to trust that love.

Chloe's arms encircled his neck, her fingers tangled in his thick hair as she reveled in the sensations that pulsed through her. She wanted to be closer. Feeling the pounding of his heart against her breasts, she wondered if he could feel hers racing. Still she longed to be closer. His heat scorched her body, his strong chest pressed hot and hard against her soft breasts. The strength of Karif's long legs held them both as she gave herself up to the raptures of her love.

His phone's ring tone shattered the moment.

Breathing heavily, Chloe pulled back, almost unaware of where she was. She knew where she had been, in heaven.

The conversation was short and in Arabic. When he hung up, he looked at Chloe.

"There's trouble at home. I'm needed. The limo's on its way to pick me up. I have to go, *chérie,* sooner than I planned."

Fifteen

"What kind of trouble?"

She resented the intrusion of the outside world. For several glorious moments, they'd been in a world of their own.

He crossed the living room to stand at the window watching for the limo. "Not everyone in Manasia was as excited about the treaty as I was. There are factions that want to keep the oil to ourselves or align ourselves with the cartel. Now that the treaty's signed, there are protests in one of the larger cities. It is not serious at this point, but I want to see what I can do to ease matters before they become more serious."

"What will you do?" Now that his departure might be imminent, Chloe was afraid. She'd known this was coming, but she wasn't ready for it.

"I need more information on the situation before I can determine how best to handle it."

Gone was the impatient lover of a few moments ago. In his place was a man of stature and power. Chloe could almost see his mind working as he focused on the problem. He was already miles away from her, his attention on the important problems now facing him from his country.

For now, she'd been forgotten. Again.

The limo turned onto her street.

He was at the door before it stopped in front of her house.

"Let me know what happens," she said following him to the doorway.

Would this be the last time she saw him? Or for another ten years?

He looked at her and nodded. "I'll call you." With a quick kiss, he hurried to the limo and was gone.

For a long time she stood in the doorway, wondering if she'd made a monumental mistake.

Turning into the house, she spied the packages on the coffee table. He'd forgotten to take the presents for his nephews and his mother.

Then she smiled. If nothing else, this gave her a reason to call him later. She could bring it over to his suite. Maybe she'd find out more about what was happening in Manasia. Was it serious enough to require him to immediately return home?

Suddenly, she silently admitted she wanted him to stay. At least for a while longer.

Chloe and Mackenzie slept in late the next morning. Fixing waffles for breakfast, Chloe took her time, enjoying the rare time with her daughter with no schedule to keep.

They talked about the previous day. When Mackenzie mentioned wanting to visit Karif's home, Chloe nodded thoughtfully. Maybe they would visit one day.

"Can I go see if Stephie can go bike riding?" Mackenzie asked after she'd finished eating.

"Tidy your room first. I want to vacuum and don't want to have to pick up a lot stuff off your floor," Chloe said.

"Aw, Mom."

"After that, you can go play."

Mumbling under her breath, Mackenzie stomped to her room. Chloe smiled at the familiar ritual. Why was it children didn't like to keep things tidy? Chloe tried to remember her own mother's admonitions to keep her room clean, but she pushed the thoughts away. She and Mackenzie were a family, it was enough.

Lingering over a second cup of coffee Chloe wondered if she had the energy to clean the entire house. Actually, what she really meant was, did she want to, or would she rather contact Karif about the packages he'd left?

"I'm done," Mackenzie said rushing down the hall. "Now can I go to Stephie's?"

"Yes," Chloe said, wishing she had some of that energy and enthusiasm.

When her phone rang she answered it before the second ring.

"Chloe?" It was Karif.

"Great minds must think alike, I was just thinking about you. I was going to call—"

"No doubt to discover further information on the situation in Manasia." His sharp tone crashed around her.

"Is it worse?" It must be for him to bring it up. Was he leaving? A clutch of dismay gripped her.

"I'll leave that for you to find out some other way. I'm mad as hell that you used our relationship as a stepping stone for your career!"

"What are you talking about?"

"Don't play innocent with me, Chloe, I'm not in the mood. I'll call you later in the week to arrange time to see Mackenzie. I think you can understand why I won't impose my company on you."

"Karif-"

He severed the connection.

Chloe held the phone for several long moments, unable to believe what had just happened.

What was he talking about? She put down her phone and hurried out to the front porch to pick up the newspaper. It must be something in the paper, why else would he have referred to her career? But what?

She snatched up the Sunday edition and stared in disbelief at the enlarged close-up of Karif she'd taken at the White House and the lead article. Anti-U.S. Demonstrations in Manasia Threaten Oil Treaty. The byline was Mike's. Quickly she scanned the article. As usual, the headline made things sound worse than they were.

Whirling she ran inside and hurried to her room to dress. She read bits and pieces as she threw on a comfortable pair of old jeans, pulled a short-sleeved cotton shirt over her head. She brushed her hair, glad its short length required so little attention.

Stopping only long enough to call Margie Anderson and ask if she could leave Mackenzie there for the afternoon, she ran to her car and headed for the *Sentinel* office.

There were always people in the newsroom. Twenty-four hours a day, seven days a week, men and women kept watch over news breaking all over the world. Today the crew was small. It was Sunday and only a skeleton staff was on duty.

Chloe found the duty editor, Sam Peters.

"Hey, Chloe, what are you doing here? Is this your weekend to work?" he asked.

"No, it's not. I want to know about the story on the front page, the one on Manasia."

"What about it?" Sam asked, "Problem with it?"

"Is Mike here?"

"No, not yet. He's monitoring that one--he'll be in later. What's the problem?"

"How did he find out?"

"Hell, how does he find out about anything? Probably came on the AP."

"Can I get a copy of the printout?"

"Chloe, what bee's in your bonnet? Why would you want a copy—"

"It's important, Sam. Where can I find a copy?"

"Look on Mike's desk. It'd take more trouble than it's worth to find the duplicate in yesterday's printouts. He probably has it there for details."

Chloe crossed swiftly to Mike's desk. It was a mess. Sighing, she began to gingerly shift papers, not wanting to disturb any order Mike might have had. Though to her it looked like scrambled eggs.

"Looking for something?" Mike asked.

"Yes, I am. The AP printout that gave you the story about the protests in Manasia."

"Why? Read about it in today's paper," Mike said

smugly.

"I already did. More important, so did Karif. And he thinks I gave the tip."

Mike shrugged. "So? It's news. You're a journalist. What difference does it make?"

"I'm a photographer. And it makes a difference. Do you have the AP copy?"

"Is the sheikh upset?" he asked slyly.

"Mike, do you have the copy?" She was almost yelling with frustration. In no mood for teasing, she rummaged through the paper piled on his desk.

"Hold on, I'll get it for you. Don't go messing up everything."

She looked in disbelief at the chaos. "How could you tell if I did?"

"Shut up. Here's the damn copy. I'm monitoring the entire situation. You'll see an update in tomorrow's paper."

"Fine with me. I just need to prove to someone that I wasn't the one to give the story."

"Hey, that's your job. You're supposed to report news tips to the paper."

"This is something entirely different. And you didn't need me for this one, you had AP. See you tomorrow."

Chloe clutched the precious printout and headed to her car. She was going to prove to Mr. Arrogant Sheikh that he was too quick to jump to conclusions. He needed to develop some trust in her. Huh? It turned out it wasn't all one sided.

She drove swiftly to the Williams Hotel fuming all the way.

How dare he think she'd used him to further her career. If he didn't know her better, it was past time for him to learn.

Gripping the wheel she realized what she was thinking. Was it because she was giving thought to his saying he wanted to marry her?

She loved the frustrating man. She should simply admit it and see where that led her. She'd loved him all those years ago. Or loved who she thought he was.

The time they'd spent together during this visit had shown her he hadn't changed fundamentally. Granted he was a bit arrogant and incredibly strong-willed, but then a lot of successful powerful men were. And some of that arrogance could be tempered.

He still had the power to excite her more than any other human being she'd ever known. His determination to get to know his daughter was endearing. When he spoke of his family, it was with pride and affection.

When he spoke to her, it was with passion and longing. Could he fall in love with her one day? Would it be enough to have his commitment if he never did? Was he courting her only for Mackenzie or did he care for her as well?

When Chloe reached the hotel, she was shocked at the crowd in the lobby. Slowly, she worked her way through the newspapermen and TV cameramen pressing in near the elevators. The talk buzzed about the sheikh and the situation in Manasia. At each elevator door stood a guard holding back the eager reporters. Obviously, the hotel was protecting its guest.

Chloe slid into the elevator banks and reached for the

Up button.

"Are you a guest here, madam?" the guard nearest her asked politely. "I'll need to see your key."

She shook her head. "I'm visiting someone here."

"Sorry, ma'am. No one is allowed up unless they're a guest. Maybe you could call your party and have them come down to vouch for you," he said.

She nodded and turned away. Right. She had a life-size picture of Sheikh Karif bin Shakirah coming down to face this crowd just to vouch for her. He thought she was the one who started it all.

Darn it all, now what?

She moved to the house phones and requested Karif's room. As she had expected, the hotel was not putting through calls. She hung up and glanced around. Could she find the stairs? Were they guarded as well?

Just then, a cry caught her attention. Turning, Chloe spied a harried-looking young woman pushing a baby carriage while a little girl of about three was crying at her side. A small boy of about five was pulling on the woman's free hand, obviously anxious to get where they were going. The mother stopped and stooped down to comfort the little girl, admonishing the boy to be quiet. As quickly as she could, Chloe crossed over to them.

"You look as if you could use a bit of help," Chloe said, smiling sympathetically. "I'm just going up myself. If you're heading for your room, I'll push the stroller for you while you handle those two."

The woman hesitated doubt in her expression at the stranger offering help.

Chloe kept her smile and shrugged. "I'm just offering

to help. I'm a mom and I know how hectic dealing with cranky kids can be,."

"Thanks, I could use it." Straightening, the harried mother lifted the little girl in her arms and held on to the boy. The woman watched to make sure Chloe was coming as they wound through the crowd.

The mother had her key ready and the guard let them on the elevator with no trouble.

Success Chloe thought as the doors slid silently closed behind her. She pushed the carriage to their room, accepting the mother's thanks before returning to the elevator. In no time, she was on Karif's floor.

Chloe stepped off the elevator and faced the two guards standing in front of the door down the hall. Slowly she walked toward them. She didn't recognize either one. Would they recognize her? And if so, would they let her in? Or had Karif told them to bar her admittance?

They moved as one unit to block her way.

"These rooms are occupied," one said in a heavily accented English.

"I'm Chloe McDonald and I need to speak to the sheikh."

As one they both shook their heads, moving closer still, crowding her back toward the elevator.

Chloe darted to the left. The guard caught her arm and hauled her before him. The other guard took her other arm and together they marched her down the hall.

"Karif bin Shakirah!" she yelled, trying to pull away from the two strong men. She wouldn't give up easily.

"Let me go. *Karif!* It's Chloe. I want to talk to you!"

One of the guards pushed the button for the elevator.

Both silently continued holding her as easily as if she were a child. Their grips were strong-- she couldn't break free no matter how she tried to twist out of their grip.

"Karif!" she screamed. Surely he could hear her. How soundproof were these rooms?

Just as she heard the ping announcing the arrival of the elevator car, the door to the suite opened.

"Karif, I need to talk to you," Chloe yelled.

She wouldn't leave without a fight. This was too important.

Salid stepped into the hall and closed the door behind him. He motioned the guards to hold her a moment.

"I am afraid that His Excellency is occupied at the moment. In any event, I don't believe he has anything to say to you."

Sixteen

"He doesn't need to say anything to me, dammit. I have plenty to say to him! I need to straighten out a few things."

She was so angry she felt as if she might explode. She yanked her arms. The guards' grip tightened.

It was obvious by Salid's slightly bemused expression that most people didn't confront the sheikh as she threatened. But she didn't care. All she wanted was to explain to Karif what had happened, make him eat his words and admit he was wrong, that she had never betrayed his trust in any way.

"I will let him know that you came by," Salid began.

"Karif!" she called again.

She glared at Salid. "It's not good enough to tell him I was here, I want to see him!" she said between gritted teeth.

"What's going on out here? Salid, I thought you could handle things." Karif stood in the doorway to the suite, glaring at the small group by the elevator.

"I want to talk to you," Chloe called, pulling futilely against the captive hands. "Or wring your neck, I'm not sure which."

At that, both guards became even more alert.

Even Salid looked alarmed.

Karif, however, chuckled sardonically. "Threats against my person is not the best way to get in to see me."

He studied her angry countenance for a long moment, then shrugged. "Very well, I'll give you five minutes." He turned and walked back into the suite.

The guards released their hold but continued to watch her closely as they all moved down the hall. Salid indicated she should precede him into the sitting room and he closed the door behind them.

"Do you need me?" he asked Karif softly, still watching Chloe.

"Don't worry, she may talk tough, but she's not going to wring anyone's neck. Chloe's against violence."

"I used to be," she muttered, crossing the room, pulling the AP printout from her purse.

Slapping the computer paper against his chest she burst out, "Read that, Mr. Know-it-all sheikh. Then you can fall on your knees and beg my forgiveness for ever doubting me. Doubting, heck, you had me tried, convicted and condemned without even telling me what the issue was." She stormed over to the window turned and stormed back.

"On my knees?" Karif murmured softly as he glanced at the AP report.

"Groveling for all I care."

She paused and glared at him, swiveling around to pace back to the window. "I'm so mad I could spit! I hadn't a clue what you were talking about on the phone. I hadn't read the paper. Mackenzie and I had just finished breakfast."

She whirled and faced him. "How dare you think I would abuse whatever relationship we have to get a news story! Do you think so little of me as to believe I'd do something like that?"

"Chérie-"

"It never even occurred to me that the situation was newsworthy. I was more concerned about you and if you'd have to return to Manasia early. I never thought to call it into the paper. And of course, Mike thinks I'm nuts not to have done just that."

"Mike?" His attention sharpened.

She waved her hands in dismissal pacing back to stand before him. "He works at the paper, it's his story. The one he got from the AP."

Karif glanced again at the printout from Associated Press.

"You're a fine one to talk about trust," Chloe said. "Where was trust when you saw the paper this morning? You didn't even *ask me* about the article, just yelled at me and hung up. I've never given you a moment to doubt me. I've never done anything to lead you to suspect... suspect..."

Her emotions were catching up with her. She could feel the tears threaten. After all this time she couldn't cry, she just couldn't.

Turning away she crossed to the window fighting for control.

"I never lied to you. You always knew who I was, what I was. You always knew how I felt about you. I was so trusting. I gave you all I had." She couldn't seem to stop talking.

He came up behind her, his hands gentle on her shoulders. "Yes, I know, *cherie.*"

"So how could you think I would do this to you? You should have at least asked."

The tears slid down her face. She bit her lower lip, desperately trying to stall them. A sob escaped.

"Ah, Chloe, don't cry." He turned her around and wrapped his arms around her, holding her tightly as the dam burst and she gave way to the grief long bottled up.

She cried as if her world had ended as it had ten years ago. The shattering of all her hopes and dreams had been devastating. She believed so strongly in their love, only to find it in pieces at her feet. She leaned into his strength and gave way to the emotions that swamped her--feeling safe and secure in his embrace.

For the first time in a decade feeling totally safe.

Karif murmured soft words into her hair as he held her through the weeping. His fingers soothed her back, threading his fingers through her hair as he sought to ease her anguish.

Gradually the tears subsided. She leaned exhausted against him the fingers of her right hand covering her face. She knew she must look a sight. Her eyes would be puffy and red. Her nose was running.

"You went to the newspaper office to get the Associated Press report?" he asked.

She nodded against him wishing the floor would open and swallow her. She was so embarrassed. How would she ever face him again?

"Why?"

"To prove to you that I hadn't given the story tip. I never even thought about doing such a thing."

"Why was it so important to tell me?" he asked softly, his hands moving over her back, up and down over and over again.

"I didn't want you to believe I would betray you," she whispered.

"It would be no more than I deserve. I betrayed your trust in me years ago."

She shrugged against him breathing in the scent of him. It was warm and spicy and very male.

Her eyes closed, she imprinted the scent on her memory so she would always remember. She wanted to stay like this forever--even as she knew she couldn't.

"Maybe but I didn't want you to think that of me," she said sadly.

"And why was that so important, Chloe? Why did you go to all this trouble to make sure I knew the truth?"

"I want you to trust me," she said softly, not fully understanding why it was so important to her--only knowing it was.

He tilted her head back, cupping her damp cheeks with his palms, brushing away her covering hand. Lightly skimming his thumbs across her spiky lashes, he gazed down into her flushed face.

"I must look a mess," she said, giving another sniff. She couldn't look away. The passion that shone from his eyes was mesmerizing.

"I think you are the most beautiful woman in the world. I always have." Lowering his mouth to hers he kissed her.

Chloe was light-headed by the time Salid interrupted a few moments later.

"The president's on the phone, Excellency." He stood just inside the connecting door, displaying no surprise to find Chloe in Karif's arms.

"Duty calls. Stay here." He reached for a clean handkerchief and wrapped her fingers around it. Quickly, he strode to the phone.

Chloe turned to stare out the window blowing her nose and mopping up the last of her tears.

She listened idly to Karif explain that the situation had been handled in his country. A tempest in a teapot, he called it.

She smiled, finding it odd that a desert sheikh could so easily quote an English saying. Must come from his having lived in England so long. She wondered how he'd liked that country.

Then she wondered why he'd never visited the United States after leaving so long ago. There was still so much she didn't know about Karif.

"Now, where were we?" he asked, slipping an arm around her waist and bugging her close to his hard chest.

"If I ask about the protest, will you assume the worst?" she asked.

"Not now that you've cleared the matter up for me."

"It's really over?"

"I think so. Very noisy and a little damage to some property, but nothing earth-shattering. The treaty is in no way jeopardized."

"And you don't have to fly home immediately to settle things?"

"I'm scheduled for a week or two to visit in America. My last function ends tonight, thereafter I'm free. Would you have dinner with me tomorrow night? We'll find a place that has dancing. Remember how much we loved to dance in Berkeley?"

She nodded. She'd loved everything about that year-- dancing with Karif had only been one facet.

"I'll pick you up at seven."

"I'll have to see if I can get Mrs. Hanson to watch Mackenzie."

"If not, bring Mackenzie here. I'll have someone watch her."

Chloe nodded.

"Did you eat lunch?" he asked, glancing at her.

She shook her head.

"Then stay and eat here and have a cup of hot tea."

She smiled. "I was just wondering about your years in England and now you offer me tea."

"Ah, but we drink tea at home as well. Hot and sweet and strong."

"I'd like something to eat. Then I have to get home. I left Mackenzie with the Andersons and don't want her there all day."

He had Salid order lunch for them both.

They sat together on the sofa awaiting the food. Karif linked their hands and rested them on his thigh as he discussed the demonstrations in Manasia.

Their talk drifted to other topics.

He told her about his schooling in England as they ate a light lunch. He told her about the reforms and plans he had for Manasia while they sipped hot sweet tea after they'd resumed their places on the sofa.

Chloe told him more funny stories about Mackenzie--as a toddler in Los Angeles and what changes moving to the capital had made in their lives.

She'd felt at peace after her bout of tears.

That peace was now shattered as every part of her yearned for him. He'd once again captured her hand in his and the connection was totally distracting.

She thought about his fingers gliding over her skin so long ago, his mouth kissing every inch of her body. She reveled in the hot memory of the delights they'd found in each other's arms, the long sultry nights when they'd been caught up in a world of two, nothing else important but the love they shared.

She wanted that again. She wanted him to move his hand up beneath her shirt and caress her bare skin. She wanted to feel his lips against her breasts, drawing the tips into the heated cavern of his mouth. She wanted him to disrobe them both and lie down with her in a big bed or on the sofa or on the floor and make passionate love to her as he had so long ago.

The spell broke when the room-service waiter returned to gather the used dishes. Karif casually released her hand. Chloe glanced at her watch. It was after four.

"I've got to go." She stood abruptly.

For more than one reason, she had to leave. It was time to pick up Mackenzie. And time to examine exactly what was going on between her and Karif.

The tears had helped erase much of the bitterness she felt over his long-ago betrayal.

But was she ready to trust him with her heart? She

had to think things through, away from him. His presence was too distracting. She couldn't think around him--only feel. And her feelings led her right back to Karif every time.

"Until tomorrow night, then," he said reluctantly.

"Oh, you left the presents for your nephews and your mother at my place yesterday. I can bring them by on my way to work tomorrow if you like," she offered.

He raised an eyebrow. "On your way? Isn't this off the direct route from your house to your office."

She shrugged, grinning engagingly. "Close enough."

"Then yes, bring them by. Would you eat breakfast here?"

She shook her head. "I'll eat with Mackenzie, then stop by around nine. I can only stay a moment. I'll have to get to work."

He nodded and kissed her.

He walked her to the door of the suite and kissed her again.

He walked her to the elevator and, ignoring the stares of his guard, kissed her again.

"I will not accompany you downstairs," he murmured, resting his forehead on hers.

"I know. Every reporter in Washington seems to be in the lobby. I'll see you in the morning."

He kissed her one last time. When the elevator arrived, he watched until the doors closed behind her.

He felt a milestone had been reached in her coming to see him to make sure of his trust. Whether or not she admitted it, she was coming around. He felt the difference after her tears.

Smiling he entered the suite. He had the reception given by the oil companies to attend, then his time was his own.

He'd see if he could get her to take time off from work. He and Chloe and Mackenzie could spend time together during the next two weeks. Begin to build their family as it should have been built from the beginning.

His heart hardened against the memory of what his father had done, the machinations the man had pulled to keep them apart.

Karif knew that he and Chloe were destined to be together, no matter what. Finding her again after all this time, free and available, demonstrated that.

Chloe floated through the rest of the day. She let the love she felt blossom. She was happy. A few more days like today and she'd let herself dare dream of a future together. She hoped he'd wait to ask her to marry him until they'd spent more time together. Then she was confident she'd give the answer he wanted.

The concern that he wanted her solely for Mackenzie faded. He'd been wonderful, listening to her tirade, believing in her again. Holding her when she'd cried. How she relished that cherishing.

His calling her beautiful had made her feel special. Even with a blotchy face and no makeup, he'd called her beautiful. She glowed with the compliment, the warmth in her heart a wondrous thing.

Her love even allowed her to forgive the past. He'd explained the arranged engagement and marriage to

Sasela--really a plan of his father's. His father was dead now. He couldn't hurt them again.

Karif hadn't told her everything in Berkeley, but he'd changed. Hadn't he shared with her the problems with the demonstrations in Manasia? Hadn't he shared his hopes and plans for the future?

She wanted to know so much more and the days remaining before he left would give them the time to discuss everything under the sun--as they had on their long nightly walks at Berkeley. Only, in those days, their discussions had been the idealistic plans of youth to save the world. Now they could discuss their own lives and the hopes and dreams each of them held.

She hoped to meld them together and find common goals and dreams. Dare she reach out for the future and make it hers? She had the confidence now to do so. Her love made her strong.

The next morning, Chloe was on tenterhooks wanting to see Karif. She dressed early and was ready to leave for his hotel the moment Mrs. Hanson arrived. Kissing Mackenzie, Chloe grabbed the bags that held the gifts and dashed for the car. Traffic was surprisingly light for a Monday morning and she made good time arriving at the hotel a full half hour before Karif expected her.

She was humming as she entered the lobby and headed for the elevators. Yesterday's crowd was gone. The news hounds had moved on to something new. The demonstrations in Manasia had fizzled into nothing and the reporters were after fresh game.

When the elevator stopped on Karif's floor, Chloe recognized one of the guards standing by the suite from yesterday. She eyed him warily. He nodded and held open the door to the suite for her.

Smiling more confidently, she entered.

There was no one in the room. Connecting doors opened from both sides, she hadn't a clue which one led to Karif's room. Or maybe he had an entirely different suite for sleeping. She hesitated only a moment then walked into the sitting room. She was early, she knew. He'd be here soon.

Maybe one of the guards was letting him know she'd arrived.

She crossed to the sofa and put the bags there. She'd have to make sure he told her if his nephews liked the gifts from Air and Space. Mackenzie'd want to know, as well.

A small stack of newspapers was on the table. Chloe smiled when she saw today's issue of the *Sentinel* on top. Had that been done deliberately? Picking up the paper, she scanned the front page.

Mike had done a small piece on the demonstrations on the lower right-hand corner. So much for the big expose.

Her attention was caught by the large picture on the front page of the second newspaper--the headlines in large print: Another Treaty In The Works?

The *Sentinel* dropped from her fingers as she focused on the other paper. The picture of Karif was good, clear and sharp, as was the image of the woman standing in the circle of his arm. Chloe sat down on the sofa, her legs unable to hold her as a sick sensation began to spread from her stomach.

The headline read: Sheikh Karif Bin Shakirah And Lady Susan Fairchild Attend The Gala Ball Given In His Honor By The Oil Companies. Chloe reached out and picked up the paper her eyes skimming the article.

Karif had been wined and dined and feted by the large U.S. oil companies in honor of the recent treaty. His escort for the evening was Lady Susan Fairchild from London.

He'd flown his date in from London to attend the event.

She read further numb to all feelings.

"Chloe, my aide said you were here."

Karif entered through the side door. He paused when she turned blank eyes toward him. Flicking a glance at the paper in her hand, a fleeting hint of anger crossed his face before he schooled it to reveal nothing.

Chloe watched, wondering if he was as adept at schooling his features to reflect passion that probably wasn't there to begin with. She folded the paper and placed it carefully on the coffee table.

"A friend of long standing the article says," she said quietly. She'd wondered why he hadn't asked her to this event when he'd practically insisted she attend the previous reception.

"Chloe, it's not what you think. Susan and I are old friends. I went to school with her brother at St. Albans. I invited Susan to accompany me some time ago when I first learned about the dinner and found out she was planning to be in Washington at the same time."

She was numb. She knew she needed to get out.

Needed to get as far away from this man as she could before she was totally destroyed.

"It meant nothing, *chérie*. It had been arranged some time ago. She and I are only friends."

"Like your engagement when you came to Berkeley? It meant nothing. It had been arranged some time before." History repeating itself. "Yet you never thought to mention it to me? Not the engagement not last night's date."

"No, I didn't. It wasn't important enough."

"Or I wasn't important enough. You could have canceled the date," she said, finally finding the strength to stand.

"It wasn't a date. Susan's someone I've known for a number of years."

"Like Sasela?"

Karif stared at her, frustration building. "No, not like Sasela."

"You know the funny thing?" Chloe edged toward the door. Away from all she had built her hopes on since yesterday afternoon. "I thought we were drawing closer. I told myself we'd never have the same kind of problem we had before. But I was wrong, wasn't I? Nothing's changed."

"Chloe, it wasn't important," he repeated.

"You're wrong, Karif. To me, it's of utmost importance. I thought we were communicating and that we had a chance to build something. I wanted to be a part of all aspects of your life but you compartmentalize me. And I wonder if I really had any special part at all or if it was all for Mackenzie?"

She reached the door and turned to face him, her

hand reaching behind her for the knob.

"You once said you'd do whatever you had to in order to see Mackenzie," she said. "Call the president, get yourself a lawyer, because you're going to need the entire weight of the legal system behind you to get to see me or my daughter ever again. And I'll fight you every step of the way."

She opened the door and slammed it behind her. Holding herself together through sheer willpower she walked to the elevator, oblivious to the guards who watched her warily.

She ignored the passengers in the car when she stepped on concentrating on breathing, on not shattering into a thousand pieces. She clenched her teeth, holding out against the pain that pierced her heart once again.

She'd begun to believe in Karif and in her love. Now she was right back where she'd been ten years ago. She had no one to blame but herself--not that it made the pain any easier to bear.

Nothing had changed. Arrangements made were arrangements kept and none of her business.

What other arrangements had already been made that he refused to tell her? Would he have continued behaving the same way if she had married him?

Slow hot tears dripped down her cheeks. Her head held high she walked across the lobby and out into the sunshine. Deathly cold and sick at heart, she didn't even notice the sweltering muggy day.

Seventeen

The phone on her desk rang. Chloe pulled her gaze from the printed schedule she'd been studying and focused on the phone. She blinked as if coming awake after a long sleep. Sighing, she reached for the receiver before someone else answered it for her.

"McDonald," she said listlessly.

"Chloe—"

She slid the receiver silently back onto the phone base, glaring at it. Karif had nothing to say that she wanted to hear.

The phone rang again shaking her out of her lethargy. She picked it up heard his voice then dropped the receiver back. Once the connection was broken, she pulled the receiver off the hook and laid it on her desk. Glancing out of her cubicle, she reassured herself no one was paying any attention. Reaching in her purse, she turned her cell phone off.

She looked at the schedule again but couldn't concentrate. She needed to get away. She was doing no good here.

Taking time to tidy her desk, she grabbed her purse. Just before she walked away, she replaced the receiver.

She heard the ring as she crossed the floor toward Mason's office. Ten minutes later, she was in her car the rest of the day hers.

She wouldn't think about Karif she vowed for the thousandth time since she'd seen that paper that morning. She'd be grateful she found out before she'd done something foolish--like agree to think about his proposal.

Driving aimlessly around Washington, she tried to keep her thoughts channeled in directions that did not lead to the sexy sheikh she'd fallen in love with.

She refused to admit that love had lain dormant for years to be revived just by seeing him again. Her life was fine the way it had been. She and Mackenzie could manage the way they always had.

She drove into Georgetown parking near the canal. Getting out, she wandered down by the water, walking along the towpath, trying to force the peace of the setting to soothe her battered nerves.

The water flowed silently between the banks, dappled by the sunlight through the trees that flanked the canal. The path was wide and dry. Ahead of her was a jogger, a couple walking together holding hands, three teenagers laughing and jeering at one another. It wasn't crowded as it was on weekends. She was grateful for the lack of people, for the semblance of privacy.

Walking slowly Chloe tried to put things into perspective. She ached with hurt, anger boiled, regret filled her heart. From the moment she'd learned how his father had interfered, she began to hope. She listened to his explanation of why he hadn't told her who he was and tried to understand.

Despite her need to be careful, Karif had slipped beneath her guard and invaded her heart. Yet he made no concessions for her.

He made no declaration of love.

When she felt the prick of tears behind her eyelids she turned and walked purposefully toward her car. She'd cried enough for a lifetime. She wouldn't shed another tear over the man.

It was time to make plans to counter his certain claim to Mackenzie.

She had plans to make--no time for mourning a love that was never meant to be.

When Chloe arrived home a short time later, the house was empty. Mrs. Hanson often took Mackenzie with her on errands, so Chloe wasn't worried. She changed into shorts and a loose-fitting top. Walking toward the kitchen to get something to drink, she noticed the blinking light on the answering machine.

She pushed the rewind, then played the message.

"Chloe, I want to talk to you. We need to clear up this situation now before you throw away every chance we have. I thought at first you were jealous of Susan. But I don't think it's that. The plans for that reception were made long before I saw you again. You said I should have told you about it, perhaps you were correct. I looked on it as strictly business and didn't think to burden you with business matters. You looked on it differently. Call me, *chérie,* don't do this to us. Don't throw away what might be the best for both of us."

The machine stopped.

Chloe stared at it, her heart hammering in her breast.

His voice ran through her like hot wine, feathering along her nerve endings, warming her, filling her with nameless longings. She pushed the rewind button, listened to his message again.

And again.

Don't throw away what might be the best for both of us. She frowned and played the message again. It sounded almost like Karif was pleading with her. She shook her head. The arrogant ruler of a country pleading with her? Ha, what a laugh. Yet--

She played it once more. His tone was cajoling, though traces of the familiar arrogance came through.

She spun around and headed for the kitchen. She refused to be seduced by his sexy voice. She knew when to cut her losses. Rubbing her aching chest absently, she poured herself a glass of lemonade. He'd be gone soon.

And sooner or later this constant ache in her heart would fade. It had before. It would again.

Karif gazed out the window at the darkened city. The nights were the worst. Alone, with only his thoughts, Karif thought of Chloe constantly. He'd tried to woo her slowly knowing she wasn't ready for the instant response he'd felt when he'd seen her again.

If they had done things his way he'd have spent every moment with her from that day he saw her on the White House lawn. He wouldn't have let her out of his sight for a moment.

But he'd gone slowly for her sake. And look where that had gotten him.

He thought of Mackenzie. She was so adorable. His heart swelled with love whenever he thought of her. He'd already dreamed of her in his life. He wanted to know what she was afraid of and what her favorite games were. What were her favorite foods and if she liked to read. He wanted to bring that enchanting smile to her face--the one that reminded him so much of Chloe yet was Mackenzie's own special smile. He wanted to feel her small arms around his neck and hear her childish giggles.

Did she know she could depend upon him in the future?

He had to reach Chloe, for his own sake and for Mackenzie's.

The days were not much better. His ministers returned home. Even the guards had been dismissed. Only Salid and Fahim remained. Few people in Washington knew he had stayed. None knew why.

Not that it seemed to be doing any good. Without the pressing business matters to fill his days they were as empty as the nights.

Karif stood in the rotunda of the Capitol and looked around at the dozens of Americans viewing the structure. He was doing a little sight-seeing, ostensibly the reason he'd stayed. He did enough each day to keep Salid and Fahim from questioning the reason for their remaining. But he wasn't enjoying the sights as he once thought to.

Moving outside to stand on the steps of the marble building, he glanced down the Mall, toward the Washington Monument and Lincoln Memorial. To his left down the Mall was the National Air and Space Museum. His eyes were drawn to it as his memory played back that day. That was how he should be seeing Washington--with Chloe and Mackenzie, not alone with only his thoughts to keep him company.

Frowning, he started back . Fahim awaited with the limo a block away. Might as well go back to the hotel. He wasn't seeing anything here.

Chloe.

Every time he called, she hung up without saying a word. He went to her house and found it empty, her car gone. The messages he'd left on her answering machine hadn't elicited a single response.

Had she even listened to them? Or once she heard his voice, had she erased them?

Did Mackenzie wonder where he was, why he hadn't been back to see her? He toyed with the idea of following through on the threats he'd made when he'd first realized he had a daughter--to do whatever necessary to see her.

But he wouldn't.

Not yet, anyway.

What he needed to do is put an end to Chloe's stubbornness. Outside of kidnaping them and taking them both to Manasia, he didn't have a clue what to do. He fantasized about her in his home. He could keep her there until Chloe agreed to listen to reason, to see that what they had was too precious to throw away.

He had the power to do that--but he never would.

He wanted her to come to him because she wanted to be with him as much as he wanted to be with her. He needed her to choose to love him again.

Walking with renewed purpose, Karif reached the limo. He wasn't giving up on Chloe. Not after all this time. He wanted her more than anything he'd ever wanted. This time, he meant to have her.

"Is the heat getting to you like it is me?" Elsie Hanson asked Chloe when she reached home that afternoon.

"It's muggy, isn't it?" Chloe said listlessly. Her hair had curled wildly in the humidity that blanketed the city. Even the air-conditioning in her car couldn't keep up. Thankfully, her house was a cool oasis in the midst of the heat wave.

Oasis. Was everything going to remind her of Karif?

"You look pale, dear, is everything all right?" Elsie asked.

Chloe summoned a smile and nodded. "I'm not sleeping too well. I'll be fine."

Elsie nodded as if confirming a suspicion and began gathering her things. "Mackenzie seems to be suffering the same complaint."

"What do you mean?" Chloe asked.

She knew her daughter was upset they hadn't heard from Karif, but she thought Mackenzie would get over it quickly. It didn't look as if that was the case. Her heart ached for the pain Mackenzie must be experiencing.

"She's been listless and depressed. Stephie called several times before Mackenzie agreed to go over. Even then she didn't seem very enthusiastic."

"I'll talk with her," Chloe said, wondering what she could say to make things better.

"I started the casserole. It should be ready in another half hour. You know, Chloe, I'm very fond of both you and Mackenzie. If you ever need someone to talk to, I would be honored to be the one you turned to," Elsie said hesitantly, worry evident in her gaze.

Chloe felt a rush of gratitude and love for her neighbor. Giving the older woman a hug, she smiled. "Thanks, Elsie, I know that. I love you, too. But this is something that talking about won't change. I'll be all right."

"Of course, my dear. I'll see you in the morning." Patting Chloe's cheek gently, Elsie turned to leave.

"One of these days, I will be all right again," Chloe vowed as she turned toward her bedroom, anxious to get out of her work clothes. "I'll recover from this as I did last time."

The thought didn't give her much comfort as she began to believe she'd never fully recovered from Karif's leaving a decade ago.

This time it would be different. She'd go on dates, find a mate, build a life that was satisfying.

Satisfying? Who wanted satisfying after they had reached the heights with Karif?

"I *will* get over this!" she said through clenched teeth as she rubbed the ache in her chest again. One day--if she lived long enough.

That night, sleep proved as elusive as it had every night this week. Tonight, Chloe's thoughts were on Mackenzie and her bewilderment that Karif hadn't called or come to see her.

Chloe hadn't liked telling her that she ought not plan to see him again. Mackenzie demanded to know why. From the shy hesitant little girl that had first spent time with him, Mackenzie had developed love for her daddy that was perfect. Now Chloe felt worse than ever knowing she was keeping them apart.

But only until Karif contacted attorneys or pulled some strings somewhere to get visitation rights. She held her breath for a long moment. He wouldn't try for full custody, would he? He said he wanted to see Mackenzie grow up, but surely occasional visits would be enough. He could *not* have her daughter!

The hum of the air conditioner didn't soothe her as it often did when she awoke in the night. Turning her head she saw it was after one in the morning. Too late to still be awake when she needed to get to work early tomorrow. Closing her eyes, she tried to relax.

The telephone shattered the silence.

"Not now," she groaned, snatching the receiver before it could ring a second time.

"Hello?"

"Chloe, it's Paul."

"I'm not on call tonight, Paul. Todd is," she said, lying back against the pillow. Not that she wouldn't relish an assignment. If she was going to be awake, anyway, she might as well be doing something.

"I know. We're on our way to a call. But I thought you'd want to know about this one. It's a hotel fire, at the Williams Hotel. Isn't that where your friend is staying?"

"Oh, no!" Chloe sat up, gripping the phone as fear poured through her.

"How bad?" she asked, throwing off the light sheet and standing.

"We're on our way. It's bad from what the reports said, sounds like the whole building is going up. There're already reports of fatalities."

Oh, please, not Karif!

Chloe hung up the phone, counted to three and snatched it up again, dialing Elsie.

It rang and rang. "Answer, answer," Chloe chanted as she waited impatiently. Taking a deep breath, she tried to calm her rioting senses. She wanted to scream. Answer the phone, Elsie, answer the—

"Hello?"

"Elsie, I need you. I have to go, can you come to be here for Mackenzie?" She was almost frantic.

Karif, get out of the hotel safely. Oh don't let anything happen to him!

"I'll be right there, Chloe."

Throwing on jeans and a loose top, Chloe felt the seconds ticking by at an alarmingly rapid rate while she hunted for tennis shoes. She found one but where was the other? There. She thrust her feet into them, grabbed her purse and ran to the living room. Throwing open the door, she was relieved to see Elsie hurrying across the street, wearing her nightgown with a robe thrown around her shoulders.

"What is it?" she asked softly as she walked swiftly up the walk.

"Karif's hotel's on fire. I've got to get there. Thanks, Elsie, I don't know when I'll be home," Chloe said, giving her neighbor a quick hug and running for her car. In only seconds, she was speeding toward downtown.

Even before she reached the hotel she saw the flames. The bright yellow and orange light shed a surrealist glow over everything. The closer she got, the worse it became.

The streets surrounding the old hotel were blocked

off. She parked her car where she found a spot and ran down the sidewalk. When she reached the police barrier, she paused only a moment. Somehow, she'd brought her camera from the car. She tried for a shot of the building, but her hands were shaking too badly. Lowering the camera, she watched, sick at heart, fear deep and insidious. The top five floors appeared to be engulfed in flames. She felt the heat from where she was, still almost a block away. As she hesitated, she heard the sound of breaking glass as yet another window exploded from the intense heat.

She counted six large fire trucks, their engines rumbling as they pumped water in arcs high against the side of the burning building. She could scarcely breathe. The top five floors, she counted again. Karif had been on the second to the top floor.

Oh, please, please let him be all right.

She slipped beneath the barrier and began running toward the building.

"Hey, you can't go there." A cop grabbed her arm.

She shrugged him off and flashed her press badge. "Press, I'm not going to get in anyone's way."

"No one goes in."

"I do." She jerked free and ran. Careful to stay out of the way she worked her way closer to the building. Flashing red lights bathed her face. Ambulances were lined up near one of the entrances to the hotel. Even as she watched, paramedics brought out two people, hunched over and coughing. Another team brought out a body completely wrapped in yellow plastic.

Chloe moved closer. The noise was awful, the crackling of the flames, the pumps on the engines, the yelling voices of the firefighters, the piercing wail of the siren as an ambulance pulled away.

Karif. Please be safe.

What would she do if something had happened to him? How would she live her allotted days if he wasn't in the world with her? She loved him so much and had thrown away their chance at happiness just as he'd said.

Oh, please, please keep Karif safe! she prayed, trying to see what was happening, to find someone who could tell her what she needed to know.

Fear as never before captured every inch of her. She'd been so blind--would she ever have a chance to make it up?

She loved him. Nothing else mattered. They could work things out. Different countries, different life-styles, different ideas of what was important and what was not, all could be worked out, if they only had the chance to do so.

"Is everyone out?" she asked the nearest fire fighter.

"Ask the captain." He nodded toward a man surrounded by the press.

Pushing her way through, Chloe confronted the man as he started to turn away. "Is everyone out?"

"No, we're still evacuating. I've given the most recent update. I'll keep you informed as we learn more."

"What about the next to the top floor? Did everyone on that floor get out all right?" Chloe grabbed his arm.

He looked down at her. "I don't know where everyone is from, lady. The hotel staff tried to go room to room before the flames engulfed the floor. I don't know who got out and who didn't. The hotel manager has names. He's checking each guest as they come out." He turned away, directing another fire fighter to the heart of the blaze.

"Chloe?" Paul asked, coming up beside her.

"Oh, Paul, thank you for calling me. This is awful. I don't think I've ever seen anything so bad. Do you know if the sheikh got out?"

He shook his head. "I don't know. I do know that there are still some people inside. The firemen are doing all they can to get them out. Come on over here. Todd's here."

Chloe couldn't look away from the hotel as Paul led her to the side, out of the way of the men fighting the conflagration.

Her heart, her love, might still be inside that burning building. She couldn't believe that Karif might be dead-- but no one seemed to know one way or the other.

How could she not have given him a chance to explain? How could she have consigned them to living life apart? Nothing mattered but that they be together.

Now that she realized it, was it too late? Had this been fate's cruel joke, to have her understand the special bond between them only when it was too late?

No! Karif had to be alive. She'd know if he was dead. She'd be dead, too, if he was gone. She would have felt it inside. He had to be alive.

A paramedic emerged from the entrance half carrying a large man. The man was coughing, tears flowed from his smoke-stung eyes. The paramedic slapped an oxygen mask over the man's face, trying to ease the discomfort of too much smoke. Chloe recognized him. Pulling away from Paul she ran over.

"Salid. Are you all right? Where's Karif?" She grabbed his arm, alarmed at how awful he looked.

"This man needs a hospital. Severe smoke inhalation. Move away, lady." The paramedic led Salid toward a waiting ambulance.

"Where is Karif?" Chloe asked again.

Salid shook his head, wiping futilely at the tears. "I do not know. We were assisting in the evacuation. Then I couldn't see him. The smoke's very dense. I should have stayed closer to him. He's my responsibility." He was racked by coughs.

"Is he safe?"

"I do not know." Salid climbed into the ambulance. Another injured man was placed inside and the door slammed shut. The wailing siren began as the ambulance dashed away to the hospital.

Chloe's fear rose.

He had to be all right, she repeated like a mantra. He had to be all right.

She moved out of the way as another fire engine pulled in close to the hotel. Shattered glass crunched beneath her feet. She scanned everyone's faces looking for the beloved face she was so afraid she would never see again.

"I need a stretcher over here."

Her eyes swivelled at the call. She watched as two paramedics ran over with a collapsed stretcher. In only seconds they were pushing it toward the ambulance. One paramedic working on the injured man even as his partner pushed.

Chloe intercepted it just before it reached the ambulance. Her heart dropped. Karif!

The oxygen mask over his face didn't hide his identity. The angry burn on one hand demonstrated clearly how close to the searing flames he'd been. Tears sparkled in her eyes. At least he was alive.

Loading Karif into the waiting ambulance, one of the paramedics made to close the door. Chloe darted inside.

"Hey."

"He's my fiance. I'm not letting him go to the hospital alone!" she said, wedging herself around the other attendant and sitting on the floor in the front of the compartment, near Karif's head.

With a shrug, the man slammed the door and they were off.

"How is he?" she asked, her eyes never leaving Karif.

"Smoke inhalation, burns on his arm and chest. It could be worse," the medic responded as he worked on his unconscious patient.

Chloe reached out and touched Karif's shoulder, leaving her hand against him, needing the contact with his warmth to convince herself he was still alive.

Time stood still. She didn't move, only willed whatever strength she could into Karif's body.

Fight the smoke, darling, she prayed. *Fight the damage done to your skin. You'll be fine. You'll be fine.*

"If you'll wait over there we'll call you," the nurse told Chloe when Karif was wheeled into the emergency room of George Washington Hospital.

Chloe wanted to stay with Karif, but it was clear they wouldn't allow that. She reluctantly went into the waiting room.

Sitting was impossible. She walked to the wide windows and looked out over the night sky. In the distance the glow from the fire was clearly visible. She walked back to the corridor. No one paid any attention to her. Would they remember she was still here?

Slowly pacing around the room her thoughts tumbled over and over.

She loved Karif. No matter what was between them she had to tell him. She would take whatever he offered. She wanted to be a part of his life no matter how small.

What was taking so long? Was he still in that cubicle or had they already sent him up to a room? If someone didn't come in pretty soon and let her know she was going into the heart of their precious emergency room and demand answers.

"Miss?" The nurse was at the door.

"Yes? How is he?" Chloe hurried over.

"He'll be okay. We'll be taking him upstairs in a few minutes. Can you help me fill out the paperwork?"

"Yes. Then can I see him?"

The relief was marvelous, washing through her, renewing her. He was safe. He'd be fine. She was going to see him in only a minute.

"Once he's in his room."

"He'll want a private room," Chloe said as she walked with the nurse to the admitting office.

"Can he afford that?" the nurse asked, pulling out the admitting forms.

Chloe smiled. "Nurse, he could buy and sell this hospital four times over. He can surely afford a private room for a night or two. Do you also have another patient called Salid? Karif would want Salid to have a private room as well."

"I'll check. Now I need particulars."

Chloe provided everything she knew. When next of kin was asked, Chloe named herself.

"We're to be married," she explained, hoping it was true. Hoping Karif hadn't changed his mind.

She needed to make sure he listened to her, make sure he knew she had been wrong to storm out as she had, wrong to refuse to pay attention to his explanations.

He had to understand that tonight had changed her perception of everything. Life was too short and too precious not to grab any opportunity with both hands when it presented itself.

She had a feeling that Karif would give her the chance she'd refused him. He could afford to be generous to her if he still wanted her. And she couldn't afford to let him think she didn't want him. She had to tell him she loved him and let him make the final decision. She'd fight him to make sure the decision was the one they both wanted.

The nurse picked up the phone and made arrangements for Karif to be transferred to a room.

"You can see him for a little while. I'm not sure he'll be awake."

"But he's going to be all right?" Chloe needed reassurance.

"So the doctor said. The smoke inhalation was severe, he's on oxygen. The burn turned out to be only second-degree, painful, but not life-threatening. Apparently, he's some kind of hero. He saved the lives of an elderly couple."

Riding up the elevator Chloe thought how like him to risk his own life to save someone else's. That was the young man she'd known in Berkeley. He'd probably thought himself invincible. At least tonight he had been.

She smiled for the first time since receiving the phone call about the fire.

Eighteen

Chloe paused at the door to Karif's room taking a calming breath. He had to be all right! She slipped into the room and eased the door shut. The noise from the hall was muted. The room was dim, quiet, still.

Dawn was just beginning to lighten the horizon. The small light near the bed gave enough illumination that Chloe saw Karif lying still in the high hospital bed. He wore an oxygen cannula beneath his nose. His left arm was on top of the sheet, wrapped in bandages clear to his shoulder. Even in sleep, he coughed.

She stood by the bed her heart flooding with love. Thanking God that he had been spared, she feasted her gaze on his face, tracing each beloved feature from his strong jaw and chin to the chiseled cheekbones covered by the taut skin tanned by the desert sun.

She wished she could see his dark eyes again. She always felt as if she were lost in a velvet midnight when he looked at her.

Gently, she reached for his right hand, holding it in both of hers and cradling it against her breasts.

His eyes opened and he stared straight into hers.

"How do you feel?" she asked softly.

He took a deep breath and coughed harshly, his face contorting with the effort.

"I have felt better, *cherie,* how long have you been here?" He moved his hand in hers until he could link with her fingers.

"As long as you have. I went to the hotel and ended up in the ambulance with you."

He tugged her hands until he brought them to his face, kissing each finger.

He still wanted her.

She breathed a sigh of relief. "I love you," she said.

"I love you, I always have," he replied simply.

She blinked. "You said you wanted me. You never said you loved me."

"Not only do I want you, I need you, Chloe."

"Oh, Karif, I was so stupid to become upset about your English friend. I should have let you explain. But I was so afraid of being left behind again like last time."

"So you ran away instead? I don't quite see the difference. We were still apart," he remarked.

She frowned a bit . "Put that way there was no difference. You're a hero, you know."

He made a dismissing gesture. "Is Salid all right?"

"He's here in the hospital somewhere. I told the admitting office to make sure he had a private room. If you like, I can go look for him when you kick me out. He was worried about you."

"Kick you out? I'm more inclined to drag you into this bed with me. You've changed a lot from the wide-eyed teenager I fell in love with ten years ago. Kicking you out is not in my plans."

"I was so afraid you--" She trailed off, tears threatening as the relief of knowing he was safe pushed down all barriers. She took a deep breath.

"I'm fine." He coughed again. "Or will be as soon as I get this smoke cleared away."

"Does your arm hurt?"

He glanced at it in surprise. "No. Did I get burned? It's totally numb." He tried moving his fingers but there was no feeling.

"Second-degree burns, I was told. Not life-threatening." She edged her hip onto the bed, her hand tightly wound around his.

"Saving those people could have been, though," she said.

"They were old, scared, and confused. I'm still young and healthy. I couldn't leave them behind."

She nodded. Karif was a man she could trust to risk his life to do what was right even for strangers and to care for those less fortunate.

How much more would he care for her and Mackenzie, people he loved?

He moved their linked hands behind her, using the leverage to tumble her against his chest.

"Your arm," she protested, trying to keep from touching it.

"I do not want you on my arm. I want your mouth against mine." He pressed her again and she complied joyfully reaching for him.

Their kiss was hot and deep. She could smell the smoke that still clung to him. Taste it in his mouth and yet still taste the sweetness that was Karif.

He broke the kiss too early, having to cough again.

"Damn."

She smiled, brushing the thick hair back from his forehead.

"It'll pass. As soon as you get released, we'll go back to my place. I'll take good care of you."

"As soon as I get out, I want to take you and Mackenzie home with me. It's past time my family met you. We can be married as soon as we reach Manasia."

"I don't have a passport."

"What's the point of being friends with the president of the United States if he can't help us out with an instant passport or two?" Karif said arrogantly.

Chloe smiled. That sounded more like him. "Then there's Elsie Hanson. She's the closest thing to a mother I have. She would want to see me married."

"Fine, she can come to visit."

"And the Andersons, Mackenzie will miss Stephie so much." Chloe began to realize what marrying Karif would fully entail. "And my work."

"I'll charter a plane, everyone you know can come over for the ceremony, stay a week and enjoy my country. You and I, however, will be on a honeymoon for two."

"I don't know. There is so much to be decided. Where we would live. Mackenzie's schooling. We don't speak your language. School would be difficult there. And I still have my job."

"We can work everything out--trust me on this, *cherie*. We'll spend the summer in Manasia. Then we can decide what to do for Mackenzie's schooling. We can decide about your job while we spend the summer getting to know each other again. Maybe you'd like to change your focus from photojournalism to filming subjects for books. We don't have to decide to today. We have our whole lives."

Chloe shook her head.

"It's a perfect plan. Stephie can keep Mackenzie company while you and I spend some time together. I'll take you out into the desert where we can be alone beneath the warm sun. We'll find a lush oasis and fill our days discovering all we can about each other. And at night we will make love until the bond is so strong nothing will ever sever it in this life or the next."

Her heart lurched but she gave him a sassy look. "All this is predicated on your asking me to marry you, of course."

The teasing lights died from his eyes. "Chloe, I love you. I would be most honored if you would become my wife."

She swallowed tears threatening again. "I love you, too. And it is I who would be honored. Yes, Karif, I would love to marry you."

He kissed her again, threading his fingers through her soft curls, relishing the weight of her against his chest.

When his coughing again broke up their kiss, Chloe lay snuggled against him, content the feel of his strong body beside hers. She'd been so afraid she'd never be this close to him again. She shuddered thinking about the fire.

"I've loved you for ten years," she said softly. "I tried to forget you, but I never did."

"And I love you, *chérie*. For a number of reasons but the primary one is that you complete me. Before I went to Berkeley I was always known as the son of sheikh Abdul bin Shakirah, wealthy sheikh of Manasia. In England I attended school with the sons of dukes and earls. In France I attended the upper academy of the wealthy and privileged.

"Berkeley was a new experience for me. New, exciting, democratic and very very different from anything I'd known before. For the first time, I found people liked me for who I was, not who my father was. A woman loved me for myself, not my title or my money or my position. It was a heady experience. One I never forgot."

Chloe listened to his sexy voice, giving in to the sweet sensations it brought, enjoying the shimmering waves of happiness that washed through her.

"I never thought of your life from that angle. I guess that explains why you didn't tell me who you were. You'd never have truly known if I loved your money or you yourself."

"In your case I believe I would have known. I missed you so much when my father had me return home and commanded me to stay. I left part of myself with you."

"While I missed you most dreadfully after a while I did have Mackenzie. She's been my joy since the day she was born," Chloe said. "You'll love her."

"I already do. I love you and I love our daughter. I

hope we will have many more children to love. But for the others I want to be there to see you pregnant, share that experience with you. See our children nurse at your breast. Watch them grow up together. Then grow old together with you."

"I wish-"

"*Chérie,* the past is behind us and gone and there's nothing we can do to change it. Let us look only forward from this day. Our lives together begin this day. We'll have no regrets, no guilt. We'll start our lives with joy and love and build on that."

"Yes, Karif. Yes." She kissed him briefly.

"Now, find the doctor and see how soon I can get out of here. Find out where Salid is. If I am to remain another day, I want to see Mackenzie. I've missed her these last few days and need to see her. And I don't want her worrying that my injuries are more serious than they are. Seeing me will assure her I'll be fine. And we want to share our news with her. Do you think she'll be glad?"

Chloe sat up and stared at him.

"I can see you are going to try to dominate this relationship from the beginning. But you need to know I'll only stand so much. I'm not one of your minions to order around. You're in my country, buster, and we don't jump to commands by mighty sheikhs."

He laughed. "We'll have a wonderful life, *cherie,* but it wouldn't hurt you to have some awe for your husband."

She grinned and brushed his lips with hers again. Her heart was bursting with happiness as she stared into his dark eyes.

"You'll just have to settle for love."

More Books by Barbara McMahon

Cowboy Hero
Cowboy Hero Series
The Cowboy Next Door
Cowboy's Bride
One Stubborn Cowboy
Crazy About a Cowboy
Never Doubt a Cowboy
Cowboy Marshal
Summer Cowboy
Second Chance Cowboy
Movie Star Cowboy

Cowboy Heroes Boxed Set Books 1-3
Cowboy Heroes Boxed Set Books 4-6
Cowboy Heroes Boxed Set Books 7-9

The Harts of Texas Series
Rebel Heart
Tangled Hearts
Reckless Heart

Harts of Texas Box Set: Books 1-3

Ultimate Billionaires Series
The Cynical Sheikh
Falling for the Sheikh
A Sheikh of Her Own
The Unforgettable Sheikh

Ultimate Billionaires Box Set Books 1-2
Ultimate Billionaires Box Set Books 3-4
Ultimate Billionaires Box Set Books 1-4

Rocky Point Series
Rocky Point Legacy
Rocky Point Reunion
Rocky Point Promise
Rocky Point Hero

Rocky Point Inn
Rocky Point Dawn

Rocky Point Boxed Set Books 1-3
Rocky Point Boxed Set Books 4-6

The Talmadge Sisters Series
Letters to Caroline
Michelle's Marriage Deal
Trusting Abby

Tropical Escapes Series
Island Rendezvous
Come into the Sun
Island Paradise

Destination Romance Boxed Set

Sweet Romance Stand-alone Collection
Because of You
Cowboy Charade
I'll Take Forever
Jared's Promise
Mail Order Bride
Not Really Married
Sweet Meant To Be
The Cowboy Comes Home
The Paper Marriage
Trusting Jake
The Banished Bride

A Sweet Clean Christmas Romance Collection
The Christmas Cop
The Cowboy's Special Christmas
A Soldier's Christmas
A Teaspoon of Mistletoe
The Christmas Locket
A Key West Christmas (*coming soon*)

Love And All The Trimmings